WHEN THE MERMAID SINGS

Helen Hollick

TAW RIVER PRESS

WHEN THE MERMAID SINGS

A Jesamiah Acorne short read Voyage of Adventure

New edition, recharted from the original publication, with additional content

Original edition published by
Silverwood Books Ltd
(sBooks) 2017

*All characters are purely fictional and exist only within the author's
imagination and the chapters of this story.*

ISBN-13:
978-1-8381318-6-9 (paperback)
978-1-8381318-7-6 (ebook)

Published by Taw River Press
https://www.tawriverpress.co.uk

PRAISE FOR WHEN THE MERMAID SINGS:

"Ms Hollick has skilfully picked up the threads that she alludes to in the main books and knitted them together to create a Jesamiah that we really didn't know." Richard Tearle *senior reviewer, Discovering Diamonds*

"Captain Jesamiah Acorne is as charming a scoundrel as a fictional pirate should be. A resourceful competitor to Captain Jack Sparrow!" Antoine Vanner *author*

"Helen Hollick has given us the answer to that intriguing question that Jesamiah fans have been aching for – how did he start his sea-going career as a pirate?" Alison Morton, *author*

"I really enjoyed the insight offered into Jesamiah's backstory, and found the depiction of our teenage hero very moving." Anna Belfrage, *author*

"I loved this little addendum to the Jesamiah series. I always had a soft spot for the Lorelei stories and enjoyed that the author cleverly brought her over from the Rhine valley to fit into the story." Amazon Reviewer

To all Jesamiah's fans.
Without your enthusiasm, the Sea Witch would not be continuing
to sail so successfully.

A DISPATCH FROM THE AUTHOR

When the Mermaid Sings was originally published by SilverWood Books Ltd of Bristol, England, in 2017. It was intended as a short read introduction to Jesamiah Acorne's world of eighteenth-century voyaging – a taster for the main, *Sea Witch Voyages* series. As an e-book only format, the text had to be limited to no more than forty thousand words, which was manageable, but left out some scenes that I had wanted to include. So, in 2021, having established my own independent Taw River Press, I obtained the rights back and decided to re-insert all the bits I had previously deleted. The result is the same story, but more of it... and also published in paperback, with a splendid new cover. I'm pleased with the result, I hope Jesamiah fans are as well!

~ WEIGH ANCHOR ~

From the time when Time was young, legends sprang from the people who told the tales of the past. Legends of hope and heroes, of hatred and enmity. Legends of devils and gods, of strength and courage, cruelty and cowardice. Of life and love, bitter jealousy and grieving loss.

One such legend was of Lorelei, a daughter of Tethys, the Spirit of the Sea. When Lorelei fell in love with the King of the Earth, she turned away from her mother and became mortal so that she could be his lover. But jealous, Tethys rose up in a storm and swallowed the land and the palace where the king lived, taking his life and the lives of many others. The people who survived, but who had lost everything, blamed Lorelei and cast her out. With her belly swelling from the child she carried, she wandered the shore, hoping her love would somehow return to her.

But he did not.

Again the sea came, and again, until the people grew afraid.

"The sea is angry," cried their priest. "We must offer the Sea Goddess a gift to appease her wrath." So, when Lorelei gave birth to a son, the priest took him while his mother slept, laid him in a basket and cast it adrift upon the sea. Lorelei was distraught for her second loss. Bereft of all reason and hope, she hurled herself from the cliffs and became a mermaid once again.

· · ·

On certain nights, when the moon rises and the stars are at their brightest, Lorelei can be heard singing a lament for her lost lover and son. But not until the white rainbow arcs down to caress the black sea will they return to her embrace, and their loving smiles end her lonely grief...

1

VIRGINIA, SUMMER 1708

Smoke drifted into the star-scattered sky, and across the river the acrid stench of burning wood, tar, rope and canvas trailed behind as if reluctant to leave the soot-blackened jetty. Jesamiah, three-quarters of the way between fourteen and fifteen years of age, too young to be a man, too old to be a child, stood silent, stunned and helpless, as tears trailed down his face, leaving white streaks in the smoke-grimed smudges. He had tried to save her, his beloved boat, *Acorn*, but the fire had taken hold too quickly. All he had of her – of anything now – were bitter memories to torment his mind and twist in tangled knots around his heart.

"Well, tha' be tha' then," Alistair Smallwood, the elected mayor of the nearest town, Urbanna, remarked as he turned away from the window and sipped at his glass of wine. "A vessel goin' up be allus a spectacle, eh, Mr Mereno?"

Ignoring the inferior burr of the man's Cornish accent, Phillipe Mereno acknowledged the remark with a polite nod. He was Master here now; the house, the plantation, the tobacco, the slaves. The money. All his, and if his younger half-brother thought he was going to get any of it – and that included that boat – he could think again.

"A great shame," someone else remarked. "She was a good

little vessel, but Charles ain't got no more use for her, has he? Not now he's in his grave."

Again, Phillipe smiled politely. "Indeed not, sir, and neither will I, for I have the two larger ships for the purpose of the tobacco trade. My father looked upon that sloop as a pleasure-thing for fishing and jaunts downriver. As I have no care for such frivolity, it was of no value to me." He beckoned to a servant to refill glasses, and for another to bring around the silver trays of pastries and sweetmeats.

One of the ladies present remarked, "Would not young Jesamiah have made use of it? I believe he enjoyed sailing?"

Phillipe narrowed his eyes, his nostrils flared slightly. He did not wish to appear churlish, but neither had he any intention of saying anything pleasant about his wretched half-brother. "Ma'am, living alongside the river, my father insisted we learnt the ways of the water for the safety of skin and soul, but sailing was his delight, not mine."

With the spectacle of a boat ablaze over, the men returned to their business and political matters, while the women, rustling in their silk and taffeta gowns, picked up their exchange of gossip again as if it had not been so dramatically interrupted, their fans flapping wildly against the last of the day's summer humidity and heat. From their perspective, it had been a respectable funeral for the much-admired Captain Charles Mereno, and this burning of his boat a fitting send-off for the sailor's departed spirit. Only, they were unaware that *Acorn* had not been the Captain's. She had belonged to his wife and *she* had bequeathed the sloop to their son, Jesamiah. A fact that Phillipe Mereno knew very well, but had kept to himself.

"Your brother has taken the deaths of his mother and your father within a week of each other with no show of fortitude, I perceive," the Reverend Coleman's wife remarked to Phillipe, her countenance wrinkling in an expression of disdain. "I notice he is by the water still. Has he no intention of joining us? Of course, his mother, being of Spanish blood, was not admired in these parts although the good Captain often implied she was not of the Catholic faith." She hissed the word *Catholic* as if the Devil himself would come to swallow her whole for the utterance of wicked blasphemy. "*He* will be much missed. She will not."

To save his wife from making further tactless remarks, her husband interrupted. "What will you and your brother do now, Mereno? Manage the estate between you? Although Jesamiah is a little young to assist, perhaps? I often urged your father to consider sending him away to finish his education. The new College of William and Mary in Williamsburg is now completed, I believe, or there is Harvard University."

"Indeed, sir. Unlike my own, my brother's education was most lax on occasion," Phillipe lied. "He wasted his time with the boats more than concentrating on his studies. He is also too young for university. But I agree, sending him to school would be a sensible option. One of the noted establishments in England, perhaps?" Phillipe offered a small bow to excuse himself, and kept silent on the fact that he was not going to spend a penny of money on his brother's education, or that it was a great nuisance Jesamiah could not be disposed of as easily as that damned boat had been.

Irritated, Phillipe glanced out of the window at the pathetic sight of Jesamiah silhouetted against what was left of the burning sloop. Turning, with the intention of sending a servant to fetch the boy in to do his duty with guests present, Phillipe changed his mind. He stepped out through the open doorway into the night and strode down the grassed hill towards the river.

2

What was left of *Acorn* rolled to starboard and disappeared into the water with nothing more than a final hiss of steam and a few agitated bubbles to mark where she had sunk.

"*Tck*. Such a shame. Your only possession gone up in smoke. How unfortunate."

Jesamiah turned slowly to stare with loathing at Phillipe, his figure dark against the cast of light shining from the house. They shared a father and that was all; there was nothing else between them. Nothing beyond mutual hatred.

Phillipe stepped closer, his head cocked arrogantly high and slightly to one side, his hands clutched behind his back, the very figure of importance. "You are neglecting my guests by skulking out here, Jesamiah. I will not have you shame me by your impoliteness. Return within and see to your duty."

"You bastard," Jesamiah said in a low voice, ignoring the command. "You set fire to her. You deliberately destroyed her."

"Now, why would I do that?" Phillipe jeered, waving one hand towards the river with mocking indignation. The congenial face he had shown to the guests had become a contemptuous sneer. "Why would I want you to have nothing? No boat, no home, no whore of a mother? And now no father for you to go whimpering to when you think life has been treating you unfairly. So sad to find yourself suddenly destitute."

Jesamiah wanted to hit this pompous, fen-sucked codpiece. Wanted to hit and hit, and never stop. If only he could summon the courage.

Recognising the wanting, Phillipe laughed. He had seen that look so many times before and knew this shrimp did not have the guts to fight back.

"If Father only knew what you had done…" Jesamiah cried, his anger stirring.

"Father?" The laughter increased. "It is Father's fault that the boat is gone. He ought to have ensured it passed to me, not you. If it had been mine, I need not have destroyed it. But I could not let *you* keep it, could I?"

Jesamiah clenched his fists. Almost seven years the elder, Phillipe was taller and stronger than he, and the beatings and punishments endured at his hands through the years were more than just scars on Jesamiah's body. The cruelties were seared into his mind as indelible reminders of inflicted hatred.

The sneer across Phillipe's mouth widened. He leant forward. "Would you be thinking of threatening me? We both know where that will lead, do we not?"

Relaxing his fingers, Jesamiah wiped at his face with his sleeve, spreading the tear-streaked grime of soot and smoke further. It was his only good coat, worn for the funeral. His mother had sewn it for him, embroidering the matching waistcoat with green oak leaves and tiny brown acorns. They had been special symbols for her, the oak and the acorn, for she said they brought good fortune. That was why her boat had been called *Acorn*.

The good fortune had obviously run out.

Phillipe noticed the tears; slapped his palm several times against Jesamiah's cheek. "Aw, has my little brother been mewling?" He grasped Jesamiah's chin, pressed hard into the flesh. "Tears? How pathetic."

He grinned, then lunging forward, clamped his hand on Jesamiah's shoulder, forcing him away from the river and up the slope towards the fenced area of the family graveyard. Until today, there had only been the one grave: that of Jesamiah's mother, buried there one week ago. Now, beside it, lay a newly-filled grave for their father.

"Let's show your mother, the Spanish whore, how sad you are at losing your tub of a boat, shall we?" Phillipe said, shaking Jesamiah as if he were a caught rat. "Let's visit the slut one last time before I throw you off this plantation for good. Sorenta is mine now and I do not want you here or anywhere near me, Virginia, or the Colonies. Is that clear?"

Trying to resist, to throw him off, Jesamiah tripped and fell, jarring his knee on a stone. Not waiting for him to get up, Phillipe grasped Jesamiah's black, curly hair and dragged him the last few yards through the gate in the white-painted picket fence. He pulled the boy to the side of the furthest grave, where he kicked him in the belly.

"Those wilted weeds you put here on your whore-mother's grave need watering." Grasping Jesamiah's arm, Phillipe pulled him to his knees. "Water them. Piss on the grave."

"My mother was no whore," Jesamiah countered. "She was the daughter of a Spanish Don. A fine lady, and our father's legally taken wife!"

Phillipe slapped him hard across the back of his head. "She was what I say she was. And you will call her whore. Piss, you little shit. Go on – piss!"

Too many times had Phillipe bullied and hurt Jesamiah for him to find the courage of defiance. Too many times had he paid a high price for wanting to fight back; he had found, long ago, that it was safer – less painful – to comply rather than resist. He did as he was bid; with trembling fingers unbuttoned his breeches and urinated on the mound of earth, knowing that to submit was the easiest and quickest way to be left alone, hoping his mother would understand that desecrating her resting place was preferable to the humiliating things his brother would do to him as punishment.

Cackling his triumph, Phillipe pushed Jesamiah hard between the shoulder blades, and he fell forward into the seeping puddle. Sitting astride him, Phillipe pressed Jesamiah's face into the wet earth.

"Say it! Say she was a whore!"

A knot twisted like the pain of a bullying blow in Jesamiah's stomach. For all the consequences, for all he would suffer, he would not say it. Could not! Would not! Phillipe punched him in the ribs again; tears of grief were pricking behind Jesamiah's eyes, stifled sobs choking in his throat. It hurt. It always hurt. The agony of the blows, the humiliation of the torture, the searing anguish that scarred body, heart and soul.

Phillipe pushed harder, forced Jesamiah's face deeper in the dirt; held him down. "Say it, you fly-blown papist worm-fart! Say it!"

The abuse and the degradation hurt so much, both physically and mentally. The thought that it would be so easy to give up, give in, poured into Jesamiah's screaming brain. Breathing was becoming difficult. He could die here, smothered by the soil that covered his mother's coffin and the weight of his brother sitting astride him. He could leave all this suffering and sorrow behind.

All he had to do was give in and die.

~ *Get up! Fight back!* ~ The words, a young girl's angry voice, slammed into his mind.

The weight lifted, a departing kick to the ribs and Phillipe moved a yard away, laughing.

Numb, an inner strength spreading through him, Jesamiah scrabbled to his knees, then stood, his legs, his entire body trembling as he adjusted and fastened his crumpled and stained white breeches.

Phillipe was making a lewd gesture near his crotch. "Perhaps I'll sell you," he mocked. "You would make some dirty old basket a fine bedmate, molly-boy."

~ *Fight back!* ~

The words tore into Jesamiah's mind again. ~ *Fight back!* ~

3

Rage swept in like a tsunami thundering across the ocean. A blind, red, engorged rage that overcame Jesamiah's fear, and swept aside all puzzlement about that strange voice in his head. The anger born of years of abuse erupted; his punch was crude and inept, but it hit home. Taken by surprise, Phillipe staggered backwards, the laughter choking into a bellow of angry pain as blood spurted from his broken nose. More punches as Jesamiah's fists pounded into his half-brother; his feet kicked, his knees rammed. No mercy as the whimpering bully sank to his knees, crying out in fear as Jesamiah continued to pummel him with blow after blow, after blow. Phillipe, was sobbing, pleading for mercy, but for Jesamiah there was no awareness of what he was doing, nothing beyond a desire to beat this monster to a pulp.

Hands were on Jesamiah's shoulders, pulling at him, and he became vaguely aware of a voice yelling.

"Leave it, son! Leave him! Come away! Come away! Jesamiah! Leave it now!"

Screaming his fury, Jesamiah tried to push the restraining grip aside but strong arms were encircling his waist now; he was being dragged aside, the voice repeating over and over, "Leave it, son. Leave him! He is not worth murdering. He is not worth hanging for! Jesamiah! Do you hear me? *He is not worth hanging for!*"

Nostrils flaring, the dirt sticking to sweat and tears, the intense rage subsided as fast as it had arisen. Breathing hard, his fury spent, Jesamiah gazed wearily at the tall, broad-shouldered man holding him tight by the arms. He exhaled a long, shuddering breath and bowed his head, the emotion running too high for him to be able to talk.

Halyard Calpin, his father's oldest friend and the estate's overseer, gave Jesamiah another slight shake to emphasise his words, and repeated, softer and calmer, "I know you want to kill him, but he is not worth the noose, lad."

Drawn by the commotion, servants ran from the house, followed at a more sedate pace by a few of the male guests. The women gathered, twittering their consternation within the safety of the pool of light from the house.

Phillipe staggered to his feet, his hands clutching his belly. Glaring at Jesamiah, his incensed words were muffled by dripping blood. "I will see you hanged for this!"

Mayor Smallwood stepped forward, his shrewd judgement summing up the situation. "Nay, sir," he said with a placatory smile, "this be naught but a brawl a'tween distraught brothers. No court o' law would bring an 'anging charge vor it. I suggest ye shake 'ands, get y'selves clean an' think nay more on it. Ye be both distressed, 'tas been a div'cult week, what with thy ma and pa passing within a sennight o' each other."

Although he had taken up his authoritative position as mayor for only a handful of months, Smallwood had known Charles Mereno for a long while, and had made it a personal policy to turn a deaf ear to the rumour of the man's more dubious privateering exploits. He had liked Charles, and meeting his youngest son this day, was impressed by him also. The eldest boy, Phillipe? Of him he was not so certain. An arrogant and angry young man who seemed to think the world owed him everything for the taking. Charles had not cared for this eldest son much either; his praise, his pride, had always been for Jesamiah. Smallwood suspected, assessing the situation for himself and knowing a little of the background, that it had been Phillipe who had started the brawl.

Cuffing the blood running from his nose, Phillipe glowered

at the older man. The retort that the dead woman was not his mother but his father's whore hung on the tip of his tongue, but he swallowed the words down with a clot of blood. Instead, he snarled his spite at Jesamiah.

"Get out of my sight. Get off my land, and stay off. If you come back, I will string you up myself." He gestured towards two servants. "See him gone."

As they tried to grasp Jesamiah's arms, he shook them off. "I need no escort. I have no intention of staying. But mark this: if I ever see *you* again, Phillipe, you will be the one to regret it, not I." He turned on his heel and stalked away into the darkness, no one noticing the fresh tears streaming down his begrimed face.

"Follow him," Phillipe snapped at the servants. "Ensure he leaves my property."

"I will see to it," Calpin said, indicating for the servants to attend Phillipe and the guests.

"Assure that you do or I will have you flogged," Phillipe growled, tempted to instruct Calpin to go as well, but the estate needed a manager and as much as he had no liking for his father's elderly friend, Phillipe had even less liking for taking that responsibility upon his own shoulders. His threat would be enough to save face before the servants. For the immediate necessity, dignity required addressing, as the guests gawping at the embarrassing scene were men of importance.

Phillipe attempted a rueful smile – difficult with a swollen nose, a split lip and two teeth missing. "Emotions are somewhat fraught," he said, fishing in his pocket for a kerchief to dab at his nose. "I beg you to return inside and replenish your glasses. I will join you shortly. Perhaps, Dr Penley, you would be so good as to attend me?"

4

"A sorry business," the Reverend remarked to Mayor Smallwood as his wife squeezed her large rump through the narrow door of their carriage. "Perhaps not a fitting way to send Captain Mereno off to make his confession before God?"

Smallwood touched his hat as the Reverend also hauled himself aboard, glad he had his own transport and did not need to rely on the hospitality of this odious pair. "Sorry indeed," he said, "yet I wager tha unusual ent'tainment'll be fitty vor much coffee-'ouse gossip these next foo months."

As the carriage pulled away and his own drew up, he noticed Calpin hurrying to assist, the elderly man's limp, a relic from a poorly healed wound to his thigh, producing a lopsided gait. The mayor waved his hand, indicating that the fellow could slow down.

"No need t'rush, Master Calpin. Convey m' farewells to Mereno, if'n ye would. Thank 'im for tha 'ospitality, even if'n it were cut short."

"Aye, sir. That I will."

"And t'young Mereno. Give 'im this." Smallwood felt in his pocket and produced a small coin pouch. "Ye'll be seein' 'im set safe abroad?"

Taking the money, Calpin slid it into his own pocket. "Thank you, sir. That is most generous. I will indeed see to the lad."

One foot on the step to enter his carriage, Smallwood

paused and half-turned around. "The Reverend b'lieves this business bain't no fitty way t'send Charles off t'meet 'is maker. What say ye on t'matter?"

Calpin looked the man square in the eye. "On the contrary, Captain Mereno would be most pleased. He had been waiting for Jesamiah to find his courage for many a long year."

A smile reaching his eyes as he settled into his seat, Smallwood nodded. "That be as I suspected," he said, rapping on the roof with his cane. The carriage lurched forward. "Goodnight to ye, Calpin," Smallwood called. "See well t'tha boy an' give him m'regards. He'll be most welcome t'seek employment vrom me, should 'e desire it once 'e's become a man full grown."

The matching pair of greys trotted smartly along the gravel drive, the carriage creaking and swaying. Smallwood peered out of the window, looking back at Calpin. He called, "A better choice 'n tha lure o' piracy which delighted tha lad's vather, I be thinkin'. Despite 'is insistence that 'e roamed tha seas as a buccaneering privateer."

5

___

Slumped on the edge of Halyard Calpin's bed, Jesamiah sat, miserable, his face swollen, his body aching and sore, his head bowed into his hands. He looked up as the bed's owner entered, bringing a swirl of mist from the river and a lingering whiff of acrid smoke.

He tried to think what to say, and blurted, defiant, "I would do it again! I would!"

Calpin removed his hat, tossed it onto a side cabinet, walked to another and poured two large glasses of rum. He handed one to Jesamiah. "Get that down you."

Jesamiah looked at the dark liquid. He had only tasted watered wine, not liquor, and certainly not this strong stuff. He sniffed it, and the sweet caramel scent slammed into his brain.

"It tastes as good as it smells," Calpin chuckled, sipping at his own.

Jesamiah frowned, then knocked the whole drink back in one gulp, fire burning his throat and bringing different tears to his eyes.

"Careful." Calpin grinned. "It's a strong brew."

"Now you tell me," Jesamiah gasped. All the same, he held out the glass for a refill. This one he sipped more slowly as his friend made himself comfortable in the only chair.

"So, what are you going to do?" Calpin asked.

Jesamiah merely shrugged.

"You will have to do something," Calpin persisted. "You cannot stay here."

"Why not?" Jesamiah looked up sharply, a glint of hope in his eyes. "I could stay hidden here in your house, keep out of the way."

Gesturing around the cluttered room, Calpin shook his head. "I built this cottage myself. It has this one room, that one bed you are sitting on and this one chair I am occupying. I needed nothing larger – when you are used to a life aboard a ship you only require small quarters."

Biting his lip to stop it from trembling, Jesamiah studied the glass of rum a moment before drinking the liquid down. The fire in his throat was just as strong, but more pleasant this time. Dizzy, his vision blurring a little, he looked up. "I will not go begging to him. I will not apologise."

Leaning forward to refill the glass, Calpin laughed. "I would hope not. Your father and I have waited a long while for this day to come."

In reply, Jesamiah said with angry bitterness, "If the both of you wanted the bastard beaten up, there was nothing stopping you from doing it."

Calpin set his glass aside, rose from his chair, lifted a canvas knapsack down from a hook beside the door and began putting things in it: cheese wrapped in muslin, a clean shirt, and two small tobacco pouches which he held up for Jesamiah to see before packing them away. "For selling or for barter."

He went to a seaman's wooden chest situated beneath one of the two windows, peered out into the darkness, then closed the shutters before opening the chest. He tossed a leather three-corner hat to Jesamiah. "See if that fits. It was mine – good for wind, rain or sun, that hat. These were mine also." He brought out an elegant box and opened the lid. Inside, a quality pistol, a powder horn, round iron bullets, replacement flints and the various paraphernalia required for keeping the gun in good working order. He closed the lid, slid the box into the knapsack, and added a tinderbox. "You might as well have these things, they are of no further use to me. You know how to load and use a pistol?"

Jesamiah nodded.

Calpin grunted approval. He buckled the bag and set it down beside the door. Before closing the chest, he brought out a sword and leather scabbard.

Handing them to Jesamiah, he said, "This was your father's. It is an ordinary weapon, nothing of much value, but it is well balanced and well made. It'll do as good for you as it did him." He paused and looked Jesamiah in the eye. "It was not for us to find the courage to fight back, lad – that was for you to do. You will be on your own out there in the world, you need to win your own battles."

Jesamiah answered with plain frankness. "And if I do not, or if I cannot?"

Calpin's answer was equally frank. "Then you will not survive. But you have already shown that you *are* a survivor. Those who have already been to Hell know the path back, and they can be dangerous people because they know how to survive what the bastards of life throw at them."

Tentatively, Jesamiah ran his fingers over the scabbard; he had never seen the weapon before. As far as he was aware, his father had always worn a gentleman's rapier.

"It is kind of you," he said quietly, "and I am sure this is a good blade, but…"

He paused. "I want nothing of my father's."

"Suit yourself," Calpin answered with a shrug. "Keep his things or sell them. It makes no difference to me, nor to your pa. Not now." He rummaged in the chest again. "There are these, as well," he said, handing Jesamiah a small wooden box. "Your ma gave them to me when she fell ill, God rest her soul." He shook his head, pressed his nose between thumb and forefinger to hide a sudden flood of sorrow. Dona had been a good, kind woman. A good friend. "Anyway, she asked me to keep these for your birthday. I guess she would not mind if you had them a few months early."

With a mixture of curiosity and rising grief, Jesamiah opened the lid to reveal a square of royal-blue velvet, which he carefully peeled back. Beneath it lay a gold signet ring shaped like an acorn and a matching acorn charm earring.

"I can pierce your ear. It might bring you some good luck," Calpin offered.

Jesamiah nodded. "Mama had a passion for acorns," he said quietly, sliding the signet ring onto each finger to see which one it fitted best. The middle finger of his right hand; it nestled there as if made for it. "She often told me that the oak was the oldest of trees and God's favourite."

"It saved the life of King Charles, second of that name, when he fled from Cromwell's king-slayers after the Battle of Worcester. He hid in an oak tree. Your paternal grandfather was a good friend, fled with him. They escaped to France by the skin of their teeth."

Jesamiah frowned – he had not known that. All he knew of his father's people was that they were from England's West Country. "Is it worth me trying to find this grandfather?"

Calpin shrugged. "I doubt he is still alive, and your pa never kept in touch with any English kindred." He went to the fire, poked life into the embers, swung a stewpot into place, and gave the contents a stir. "We will eat, then I will do your ear and then you can get an hour or so's shut-eye. As long as you are gone from here before dawn, you should be safe enough."

For several minutes Jesamiah sat staring at the strengthening flames and the sparks flying up the soot-blackened chimney. Finally, he admitted in a quivering voice, "I'm scared, Halyard. I only know this place. Where do I go? What do I do? How do I manage?" Biting his lip to drive off fresh tears, he looked at his muddy shoes. One of the silver buckles had been torn off, and his silk stocking had a hole in it. "And I'm not exactly dressed for travel," he pointed out, attempting a weak smile.

Nodding over his shoulder, Calpin indicated the chest. "Have a rummage in there, see if there's anything that fits you." He flapped his hand at the room and its plain furnishing. "Do you really want to stay here? Or would you rather set off to see the world, seek adventure, fame and fortune? Go to interesting places?" He winked. "Find a pretty girl to fall in love with?"

Grimacing, his face flushing, Jesamiah confessed, "I don't know much about girls."

Laughing, Calpin fetched two tin plates and wooden

spoons, and set them on the small table. "At your age I would hope not, but you will not be almost fifteen forever, Jes. There is life, love and the delight of a woman out there waiting for you. You will not find any of it here in Virginia, though." He felt in his waistcoat pocket, handed Jesamiah Mayor Smallwood's coin pouch, and explained who had donated it. "I have added some silver coins of my own. There is enough in there to see you through to the autumn fall, longer, if you sell that sword. Take care and do not spend the profits on unnecessaries."

Returning to the fire and the bubbling stewpot, he raised a warning finger. "There is not much additional advice I can give you. Choose wisely where you spend the money and keep it well hidden. Keep your wits about you, learn from those willing to teach you, trust no one until you know for certain that you *can* trust them, and even then, do not trust them. And only go with clean women. For the rest, you will need to find out for yourself."

It was on the tip of Jesamiah's tongue to ask what Calpin meant by 'clean' women, but he let the subject go.

Dressed in a warm, broadcloth boat coat, calico shirt, moleskin breeches and a pair of leather boots that fitted well enough with two pairs of woollen stockings, the gold acorn dangling from a sore and bloodied earlobe, and his belly full of mutton stew, Jesamiah was feeling more optimistic as he walked with Calpin through the dew-laden damp of the pre-dawn darkness towards Sorenta's main gates. He was leading Calpin's sturdy old chestnut cob mare and was to leave her at the livery yard in Urbanna. From there, he would find a ship to take him to Port Royal, Jamaica.

"There will be men there who knew your father and who will be saddened to learn of his death," Calpin explained, trying to think what else of use he could tell the lad. "Get yourself work, steer a course for Port Royal and ask for Captain Malachias Taylor – he will turn up there eventually. He is the one you want. He sails *Mermaid*. Last I heard she was a brig, but he might have upgraded again since then. No matter, he names all his vessels *Mermaid*. He and your father sailed many a nautical mile together."

The crickets were loud, and somewhere nearby, a frog croaked. All else was quiet. A shooting star trailed bright against the dark-blue sky. Jesamiah watched it fall. A soul crossing to Heaven? His mother or his father?

"Before everyone came, I thought I'd killed Phillipe,"

Jesamiah admitted in almost a whisper. "I don't know if I'm relieved that I didn't, or not."

"For the enemy you've now made, you might wish you had, lad, but put it behind you. Look forward to your bowsprit, not back to your wake."

Not reassured, Jesamiah asked, "What if I make a mess of things? What if I fail?"

Halyard Calpin pursed his lips and shook his head. "Your father failed at a few things, so did I, so does everyone. Your pa was successful at things, as well. He regularly ran against the law by smuggling contraband, but never got caught. He – *we* were privateers carrying a Letter of Marque that gave us royal leave to plunder ships flying Spanish or French colours. Your pa was a good Captain, knew his ship, his crew. Knew the sea, knew which vessels to attack and which to leave alone. But he messed up occasionally." Calpin patted his thigh and the badly healed wound which never stopped aching, especially when the rain drenched, or a cold wind blew in from the east. "I got this on one of those occasions, so he set me up here as his steward instead. I missed the sea at first, but soon grew used to the sounds of the land and the trees. When the wind is high and blowing through the treetops it can sound much like the sea, did you know that?"

Jesamiah shook his head.

Calpin laid a hand on the lad's shoulder, squeezed, affectionate and reassuring combined. "Go out into the world, value your honour, loyalty, integrity, and do your best. Just do your best."

They stopped beyond the gates and Calpin boosted Jesamiah into the saddle. It took him a moment to set the unfamiliar weight and feel of the sword at his hip comfortably, while Calpin checked that the straps of the knapsack were secured tight onto the saddle rings.

"Well, Jes, God be with you, son," he said, his hand on Jesamiah's knee. Calpin nodded towards the river and the pale wraiths of mist that were rising and swirling with the faint light of the dawn. "If you find Malachias, get word to me so I know you are safe; he will know how. Now, be off with you!" He cracked his palm hard, on the mare's rump and she lurched forward into a lumbering canter, Jesamiah having to cling to her mane to keep in the saddle. When he righted himself and looked back, the ornate wrought iron gates were closed and Calpin was gone.

7

CORNWALL, ENGLAND, DECEMBER 1708

The boy with the black hair had been invading Tiola's dreams again. She sat in the barn, hidden in the summer-cut hay; she often came here because the smell and the dust made her father sneeze, so he avoided the place, just as she avoided him as much as she could. Her two man-grown brothers had no care for an irritating almost-eight-year-old girl, so neither did they come searching. Carter and Bennett, nine and three years her elder, preferred to be out in their boat, fishing, unless the Cornish weather was too inclement even for them to tolerate. Her mother knew where and why she sought the solitude, but Mother knew that her only daughter took after her own mother, and respected her especial gift of Fey, and left her to the privacy of her visionary thoughts.

Tiola, named for that same grandmother, was an inquisitive child who behaved older than her years and was full of questions: what are clouds made of? Why is the sky blue? How wide is the sea? Who is the boy I see in my dreams? She had asked that last question only once. The resulting whipping to her back and buttocks from her father, the Reverend Garrick, had taught her the prudence of silence.

She sighed. Her mother was calling for her to come and help with the afternoon chores. All Tiola wanted to know was the identity of the boy with black, curly hair. Boy? No, young man now. He had been a boy when first she had watched him, but

23

last night, in her dream, she had clearly seen that he was growing up, maturing into manhood. She had watched him, in her mind, many times; felt his enjoyment as he dabbled with the gentle flow of the river and sailed, or mended, or painted his boat. Had cringed when the shadow of his brother blotted the sun, wept with him when the cruel bullying left its mark of fear and pain. She knew about that wicked shadow of fear, for her father cast the same shadow.

She had saved him, the boy, all those months ago, when he had almost given in to the grief of despair, and surrendered to the malignant presence of Death. She had shouted at him with mind-words: ~ *Get up! Fight back*! ~

But she needed to know who he was because she had to continue to keep close watch over him. Had to keep him safe. How and why, she was not yet certain, but she would find out, one day. Perhaps soon? Or maybe when she was a woman grown, and this embryonic gift of Craft that she possessed, passed from grandmother to granddaughter, was fully awakened?

8

DECEMBER 4TH 1708

Four months of plying up and down the east coast of North America, from the Chesapeake to Charlestown, South Carolina and back again. Routine: load a cargo, take it to where it had to go, unload, reload…

The monotony was broken by the challenges of the weather, from hot, sultry days where the heat-scorched breath and the deck ran with sticky tar, to downpours of rain ushered in by the tail end of the hurricane season. As autumn slid into winter and the *Anna* ploughed her way northward to Boston the bitter north-east winds blew in, with the rigging rimed by ice, and hands, faces and feet forever cold. Returning south, they were heading towards the sun of the Caribbean, short-handed by two men. One had died from blood loss after severing his hand when a cable had come loose and cut through flesh and bone as easily as a sharp knife through softened lard; the other had fallen from the masthead, breaking his neck. Both had been drunk and were not missed by Captain or crew.

Jesamiah sat cross-legged beside the longboat, taking advantage of the shade and shelter from the sun and the wind, busy about mending a sail. Despite the protection of a leather patch, his palm was blistered and sore. He paused, sucked at a new spot of blood as the needle stabbed his finger. His hands were calloused, tar-grimed and rough, his skin sun- and wind-tanned and his hair was plaited into an unruly queue. His youth was changing into manhood, his voice losing its uncertain pitch to become deeper and huskier, and his face sprouting hair. He had not washed for several days. None of them had.

He was fifteen today, although only he knew it. When he had signed on as a foremast jack, he had told the Captain, Nathanial Parker, that he was seventeen. Whether he had been believed or not was immaterial, for he was here, aboard *Anna*, with no further questions asked. There would be no birthday treats, no hug and kiss from his mother, no interesting package containing something nice placed beside his dinner plate on the mahogany table in Sorenta's lavish dining room. Thinking of his mother, after sucking the blood from his finger, Jesamiah touched the gold acorn earring dangling from his right earlobe. She had intended the trinket for his birthday today, though she would not have envisaged the day was to be spent aboard a merchant ship bound for Port Royal.

The food aboard *Anna* was poor. Weevil-riddled hard tack, over-salted stews with more fat and gristle than meat, the water in the butts had turned green and foul within days of replenishing. His worn old clothes were constantly damp and the work was hard. Sailing a ship – a brig like *Anna* – took a lot of effort. Sails had to be tended; not just altered to meet the fancy of the wind, but mended and patched. Frayed rope and cordage had to be spliced. Rigging, both standing and running, maintained in good order. Ships had to be kept watertight using oakum made out of old bits of rope mixed with rags and fibres, then coated in pitch and rammed between the timber joints and deck planks with a caulking iron. The decks needed daily scraping with the brick-like, Bible-sized holystones. Hard, bone-wearying work.

Night and day, day and night, hour after hour, week after week, no matter the weather or the weariness of body and soul.

Anna rolled as a strong gust of wind buffeted her. Jesamiah looked up, ready to assist in tending the resulting flap of the mainsail if needed, but other men were already there, seeing to it. He fashioned another stitch and grinned as Captain Parker, standing on the quarterdeck, grabbed his felt hat which was about to be abducted by the wind. Life aboard a merchantman? Tough, relentless work.

Jesamiah absolutely loved it.

"You finished that yet?" growled Stannis, the bosun, as he walked past, his gait rolling with the ship. No one knew his first name, or even whether he had one. General opinion was that, if he did, he was too mean-minded to use it.

"Nearly, sir – three more stitches an' I will've done."

"Providin' you don't take all bleedin' day about it. When your dainty 'ands 'ave done stitchin', get tidied away an' get yourself up that mast to relieve Markham. Your eyes are better 'n 'is. There's a ship layin' over t'starb'd. Cap'n as wants t'know what she be."

"Aye, sir."

Before Stannis had walked the length of the deck, Jesamiah had completed his task and was heading for the mainmast rigging. He hoisted himself up into the shrouds and began climbing, gripping on to the permanent rigging that supported the mast, not the ratlines, the smaller, tarred ropes stretching horizontally like the steps of a ladder; the bare, hardened soles of his feet scarcely feeling their coarseness as he climbed. Manoeuvring around the running gear that threaded its way through the rigging, he climbed on upwards. The view of the ship grew narrower beneath him, the great grey and tar-stained arcs of canvas billowing and cracking, banging and slapping, the roar of the wind, loud in his ears.

He reached the wooden platform halfway up and, ignoring the easier route through the lubber's hole, swung outwards up and over the futtocks and the rim of the platform. A few agile steps and he was over. The sky was the purest blue, only a few puffballs of white cloud marring its perfection. The horizon plunged back and forth with the swaying, circular motion of the mast as the ship rolled and pitched, the distant line sweeping in an unbroken arc where sky met shimmering sea. The men working below on deck were minute from up here, *Anna* herself appearing long and thin, and so small compared to the vast blue of the restless ocean surrounding her.

Jesamiah grinned at Tom Markham, who was on his feet ready to go down. Markham pointed to the black shape of a topgallant sail north-east of their course.

"That's her. She's been with us since first light. I've a suspicion about her. A smell."

Settling himself, as if unaware of the great drop below, Jesamiah answered, "Do you reckon she's Spanish or French? Will they attack?"

"If she's flying colours from either country we could be in trouble. Privateering" – Tom spat saliva into the void below – "bah, piracy more like, be fit for whatever side of the mast. We prey on them, they prey on us." He spat again, stepped onto the rigging and began his descent. "Sing out if you spot what she is. If she's an enemy, we'll need every minute we can muster to get away from her. We ain't no match for the Dons or the Frenchies, and once they see we're a poorly armed merchant, well, I hope you know your prayers, young Acorne. The safety of English Port Royal is a good few hours away yet!"

Smiling to himself, Jesamiah shuffled his backside into a more comfortable position. *Acorne.* It had been the first name to come to mind when he was asked to sign his mark on *Anna's* list of crew. He had not wanted his birth name, had not wanted anything more to do with his old home. He had decided to take on a new identity as well as a new life. The 'e' he had added with a flourish as he had signed. *Jesamiah Acorne, foremast jack.*

He was determined to turn that last into 'Captain' one day.

The sun moved across the sky. An hour, two, passed by. Jesamiah was quite happy perched here in the crosstrees. He had a book to keep him company, nearly finished – an account by Master William Dampier extolling his historic circumnavigation of the world. Glancing up occasionally, he saw that their unwanted companion was maintaining a discreet distance, but around noon, having been engrossed in a particularly interesting chapter, Jesamiah looked up to see the ship had edged closer. She was about three miles distant now, and, with a slight shift in the wind, her fluttering pennant atop her masthead was more visible. He shoved the book away into its protective canvas bag, brought out a telescope, and snapped it open.

She was a frigate. And she was Spanish.

9

———

The sense of panic was as crisp as an autumn-frosted Virginia morning when Jesamiah slid, hand-over-hand, down the backstay to the deck. *Anna* carried two swivel guns and two six-pound cannons along with an array of muskets, an unpredictable blunderbuss, some pistols and a few other hand weapons. She was a merchant vessel, not a fighting ship. Each pound weight of armament she carried meant a pound less of cargo – and profit took precedence.

The expression 'running around like headless chickens' sprang into Jesamiah's mind as he watched the crew bustling about but not doing anything productive.

"We'll never outrun 'er," one man said gloomily.

"More chance outrunning her than anything else," Tom Markham stated.

"Nay, they'll mow us down like a scythe cuttin' corn."

"Might ignore us," someone else suggested.

"We'd be best to 'eave to an' surrender," old Seth muttered through toothless gums.

"Could we not try outwitting them?" Jesamiah suggested. Everyone fell silent, stared at him as if he had suddenly sprouted a second head.

The usually grim-faced Stannis laughed, although his cackle was filled with derision. "Out of the mouths of babes," he guffawed, then swiped the back of his hand across Jesamiah's head. "Idiot."

Captain Parker, however, creased his brows into a furrow and, tilting his head to one side, said, "Explain, boy."

A faint blush tingeing his face, Jesamiah cleared his throat, and ignoring the sniggering and Stannis's growl of disapproval, launched into his proposal, although, even as he spoke, he could hear the ridiculousness of the suggestion.

"Why can we not pretend to be Spanish? They will not attack another of their own kind, surely?"

The sniggers increased to outright laughter.

"For one thing, we b'aint Spanish," Stannis sneered. "We've no Spanish colours to 'oist."

"How difficult would it be to make a flag?" Jesamiah replied. "All we need is a white background and some red material to fashion a jagged *Cruz de San Andrés*, a rough-edged red cross."

"You think that'll fool 'em?" Stannis retorted. "The boy's addle-'eaded, Cap'n. Been in the sun too long. Salt water's got at 'is senses – the few that 'e 'as, that is."

"Privateers often fool their prey with such a ruse," Jesamiah countered, growing more confident. "Why not merchantmen, if it's a way of avoiding conflict?"

"Maybe, lad, because we are *honest* merchantmen?" Captain Parker said with a half-smile.

"What use honesty," Jesamiah countered, "when you're dead – or about to be?"

Indicating the conversation should be terminated, Stannis cut the air with his hand. "We be wastin' precious time, Cap'n. We oughta be settin' all sail an' 'eadin' for the nearest safe 'arbour."

Captain Parker waved vaguely towards the horizon. "Which is at least four hours away, and, even with more sail, we will not outdistance a Spanish frigate."

Stannis persisted with his objections. "A tardy flag'll fool no one. They'll demand we 'eave to, then what?"

"Then we tell them a plausible cock-and-bull story to set them in a different direction," Jesamiah answered simply.

More laughter from the bosun. "'Ow bleedin' careless of me, I forgot me book of Spanish nautical terms!" He thrust his snarling face close to Jesamiah's. "They'll soon bloody work out we ain't Spanish when they 'ear us talkin' English."

It took an effort, but Jesamiah kept a straight, calm expression. "Then I suggest we speak to them in Spanish. Sir."

Resting his hand on Jesamiah's shoulder, Parker gave it a little squeeze and said kindly, "It was a good possible plan, lad, but alas, I speak none of their lingo."

Jesamiah returned the smile, said with assured boldness, "But I do."

With a Spanish flag hastily, if somewhat shabbily, sewn and hoisted aloft, and his grubby shirt and equally dirty breeches exchanged for his better-quality clothes which had been stored for safekeeping in his seaman's chest, and because he had grown, become a little snug, Jesamiah stood next to Captain Parker, who had taken the helm. Bosun Stannis stood a yard behind, looking as if murder was his only coherent thought. Orders had been given for every man to say not a word unless it was " *Sí, señor.*"

"You know what commands to give?" Parker queried as he adjusted the wheel slightly, his own outfit temporarily that of a helmsman.

His hand gripping tighter to the hilt of his father's sword dangling from its hanger buckled at his hip, Jesamiah nodded and licked his dry lips. He had to make a good show of this, for the sake of staying alive under Spanish scrutiny, and to prove himself to his own crew. If he failed with the latter, then the former would be a welcome end to it.

A single *whoomph* of sound, and a cannonball arced through the air from the Spaniard and plopped into the water with a plume of spray sixty yards ahead of *Anna's* bow, a clear, unmistakable signal to heave to.

Taking a deep breath, Jesamiah strolled to the quarterdeck rail, his hands clasped behind his back, mimicking Captain

Parker's usual stance. Praying that his youthful voice would not crack, he called out the orders to heave to in Spanish. Not needing a chain of instructions, the crew hopped to and shortened sail, bringing *Anna* to an efficient halt, the wind rattling her protesting rigging and aback sails, the sea rolling uncomfortably beneath her keel.

A deep breath. "*¿Cual es su barco?*" *What ship are you?* Jesamiah called across the closing gap between the two vessels, his hands cupped around his mouth to help his voice carry further, and to hide his young appearance.

The answer came back as an identical question, and a further one: "*¿Está usted un mercante?*"

Again, Jesamiah answered in Spanish: "*La* Anna. *Sí, un mercante.*" He leant across the rail, waved a clenched fist at the flapping canvas and let rip with a torrent of profane abuse and a reprimanding complaint that there were two English ships prowling in his wake. He was not pleased to be delayed by this Spanish popinjay. He then demanded that the frigate escort them safely to their destination.

The response was an equally impolite refusal.

"*¡Mierda!*" Jesamiah shouted back, adding a few more colourful expletives. "I have minimal armament, I expect you to do your bloody duty and protect me against those sodden English pirate bastards!"

The Spanish captain retaliated with something explicitly derogatory, ordered all sail set, and swept past *Anna* in a gush of spray and with not a backwards glance.

For two full minutes *Anna's* crew stood in open-mouthed astonishment, staring at the rapidly diminishing ship. Almost as one man, they turned to look at Jesamiah, who calmly gave orders, in English, to get under way.

"And not one cheer please, gentlemen. We are supposed to be an anxious Spanish crew fearful of some bloody English pirates following us."

All the same, several of the men did raise a muted "Huzzah".

Captain Parker stood aside for the genuine helmsman to take his place, then patted Jesamiah's shoulder as he nodded approval. "Well done. I will give you a generous bonus when we reach Port Royal – you deserve it. And I reckon a promotion to able seaman?"

Jesamiah touched his right forefinger to his forehead. "Aye, sir. Thank you."

"Very well, very well. Get yourself out of those fine, fancy clothes and resume your duties. I will not have lazy idlers aboard my vessel."

Again Jesamiah touched his forehead and scuttled below to change his clothes.

"Ye'll be courtin' trouble, Cap'n," Stannis growled in disapproval. "Give these young tars an inch of rope an' they'll be takin' a mile."

"I usually agree with you, Bosun, but not this time. That boy has a clear head and a sharp wit to match. All he needs is to gain seamanship experience, and then I would not like to face him in an argument on the high seas." Thought to himself, *and Lord in Heaven help us if ever he decides to turn pirate.*

11

PORT ROYAL, JAMAICA

Port Royal was not as Jesamiah had expected. Even after sixteen years, the devastation of the 1692 earthquake and accompanying tidal wave was evident. Tom Markham explained, as they walked, that, following the destruction, the survivors had fled to the opposite side of the bay to rebuild property, businesses and their lives.

"The wealthy, that is. The poorer wretches are even now living in makeshift, ramshackle huts." He pointed to several of them, proving his statement.

No one, it seemed, had bothered to clear up the mess that the forces of nature had left behind. Weed-strewn mounds marked where grand, brick-built buildings had once stood, wooden hovels and canvas shacks served as homes and workplaces for those who relied on the busy harbour for a living. A few stalls and makeshift shops selling food, mercantile and nautical goods straddled the sewage-strewn streets, with not much else beyond a row of equally cobbled-together warehouses at the end of the quay. Between it all lay a scatter of rough-built and rough-frequented taverns and brothels.

"This was a glorious place once," Tom continued as he stood beside Jesamiah, surveying the dismal sight as the sun slid lower towards evening. "Every seaman in the Caribbean used to come here. Back in Morgan's day, whenever a buccaneer dropped anchor, the whole town would turn out to see what treasure they had plundered. Even the servants and the poor were rich back then."

"You knew Morgan?" Jesamiah asked sceptically; surely Markham was only in his late twenties or early thirties? Sir Henry Morgan, the scourge of the Spanish, had gone to God in 1688, twenty years ago.

"I were eight years old the day he were buried; his funeral was a sight never to be forgotten. The streets here were crammed with mourners lined two, three, four deep. The women, tears coursing their faces, threw flowers onto his coffin as it were carried by, the men, also, openly wept. I recall my father's hand gripping my shoulder fit to break the bone, his body shaking with grief."

Tom paused, and puffed his cheeks in a great sigh. "Port Royal were something then. All this along here would've been abustle with sailors, merchants, taverners, street doxies, dock workers, slaves. The harbour so full that inbound ships had to wait their turn to drop anchor and unload. Day and night, such a business of life you never did see. Nor likely to see again. If even half a dozen ships were to drop anchor here now, I reckon you'd be lucky."

They walked in silence for a few minutes, Jesamiah feeling as if the land was rocking beneath his feet, his body not yet adjusted to being ashore. *Anna* was safely moored, her cargo unloaded and stored ready for auction, her sails neatly furled, her crew paid and her captain taken across the harbour to visit well-to-do friends at Kingston.

"The sea took everything," Markham added with a sigh at the remembered tragedy of grief. "First the earthquake hurled buildings to the ground as if a child were knocking down castles of sand, then the sea swept in and swallowed everything that were left, including the church where they'd buried Morgan. Them who did not die beneath the rubble, or drown, fled across the bay or inland. They reckon there were more than six thousand souls living here before the day the ground heaved itself up to scour the land with God's wrath. Six thousand. And most of them killed within moments, with no chance to confess their sins or pray for forgiveness."

Six thousand? Jesamiah whistled. He could not imagine that many people in one place.

"Over half died that day, another two thousand taken in the weeks that followed," Markham added. "Death stalked the rubble and the shore, taking those who were injured, diseased or starved. Men, women, children. The rich, the poor, servant and slave. When the Reaper comes, he sees nowt save another pitiful soul to claim for his own."

"You survived, though," Jesamiah said.

"Aye, but only because my uncle turned up a few days later and found me. He took me aboard his ship, took me to safety. Been at sea ever since."

As they strolled on, Jesamiah smiled at a blonde lady with a cascade of ringlets covering her bare shoulders. More than was decent of her firm, round breasts was on display. He found himself staring, intrigued and more than a little excited at their proffered enticement.

"Your father, your family?" he added, turning away from her beckoning finger and trying not to blush, nor think of what was happening in his breeches.

"Dead. Mother and five sisters all crushed by the walls of our house falling in. Pa drowned. They found his body a few days later." Markham also smiled at the blonde, but did not blush. "He were one of the lucky ones. He got a Christian burial. Most did not. They were left to rot or to feed the fishes. The sharks came in with the tides. They say that on some nights the sea still runs red with the blood of those who were torn to pieces." He felt in his pocket for the silver chinking there. "Look, lad, you go find a tavern or something. I'll set about my own entertainment for a while."

Initially not comprehending, Jesamiah felt put out that he was to be abandoned so soon in an unfamiliar place, but when the blonde offered to accommodate both of them, and Markham growled a firm, "No", his friend's intention became apparent. The blush consumed Jesamiah's face again, and clearing his throat, he walked quickly away with what he hoped was a confident swagger.

The effect was ruined entirely when he turned into a side

street and tripped over a rough-hewn step. He fell, his head striking the corner wall of a chandler's store. He sat in the dirt and dust, winded and disorientated. Blood was trickling down his face, his vision swirling in waves of red mist.

Port Royal had not given Jesamiah Acorne much of a friendly welcome.

12

The town was behind him. Sitting in the dust, Jesamiah could hear the bustle of men about their business, the laughter of children, the chatter of women. A horse neighed, a dog barked, a parrot squawked. Ironclad cartwheels rumbled. Someone shouted – he could not hear what, an indistinct voice calling an indistinct word. Hammering and sawing rasped nearby, the squeak of a pulley, the creak of straining rope.

He could smell the sweat of the slave labourers and the scent of new wood. Knew, somehow, without turning around, that a house was being built on the edge of town overlooking the harbour. A house that, mere moments before, had not been there. Too scared to look, he stared, steadfast, at the rough, sandy spit of land that ran into the sun-dazzled blue sea ahead of him. But had the sun not been heading for the horizon as he'd come ashore? He frowned, closed his eyes as a wave of nausea swept through him.

Swallowing vomit, he found the courage to open his eyes, looked again at the stretch of sand. A man appeared from out of the mid-afternoon sun-haze. A large, heavily-built man, dressed in a scarlet coat with exquisite gold braiding and silver buttons. A gold chain of office decorated his chest, and at his neck frothed a cravat of Alençon lace matching the lace shirt cuffs protruding from his sleeves. An elaborate plume of black ostrich feathers adorned his velvet three-corner hat. A stout man, with a paunch of a belly and bowed legs. He was shouting something, waving his arms, fists bunched. Was he drawing attention or trying to warn? He came nearer, striding on, his rolling seaman's gait obvious. Angry at something. His face was as red as his coat.

His eyes were narrowed, furrowed brow swooping downward as he shouted in Jesamiah's direction. "Get you gone! I want nothing more of you! If I see your wretched face again I will hang ye! D' ye hear me, Mereno? I will personally see ye hanged!"

Jesamiah's mouth tasted as dry as the sun-baked white sand. He tried to stand, but his legs felt like jellied bone marrow. Who was this man? How did he know his name? No one here, as far as he was aware, knew him as anything except Acorne. What had he done so wrong to be threatened with hanging?

He attempted to get to his feet. Half-crouching, half-standing, his head was reeling. He again fought down the urge to vomit. Shut his eyes.

A voice, very distant, a young woman's voice. Calm, gentle and reassuring.

~ Breath slow and deep. ~

Mercifully, his head stopped swimming. The rushing noise in his ears ceased. One last, slow, deep, steadying breath. He opened his eyes.

Port Royal. Evening. As it had been when *Anna* had dropped anchor. Shabby, decrepit, a hell's pit of poverty. No particular bustle of people, no sounds of a house being built. No man in a bright scarlet coat threatening to hang him. Giving up trying to control his stomach, Jesamiah sank back to his knees and spewed what was left in his belly into the rubble and dust.

13

—————

"You alright, son?"

A man was bending over him, taking his arm, half-shaking it, half-assisting him to rise.

Jesamiah looked up into a face with weatherworn, tanned skin, several teeth missing and a beard that was more grey-grizzled than the brown it had apparently once been. Bright eyes sparkled beneath a three cornered hat that sprouted a red-dyed feathered plume.

"You alright?" the man asked again.

"Yes, I think so," Jesamiah answered, scrambling to his feet. He was at the harbour – how had he got here? Three ships, in addition to *Anna*, rested at anchor, the nearest sporting a splendid figurehead with carved seaweed hair draped over her bare breasts; her fishtail curled as if clinging to the bow itself.

Mermaid.

"You sure?" the sailor asked again, his hand still clasped to Jesamiah's arm.

"Just a bit dizzy, that's all."

"Not surprising," the man said with a nod and grim smile. "That's some cut to your head. You came down quite a wallop."

Touching his fingers to his temple, Jesamiah looked at the sticky smear of blood left on them.

"I saw you take the tumble as I were coming ashore. Noticed you earlier, too, with Tom Markham?"

Jesamiah nodded, then wished he hadn't. "Aye, from *Anna* over there." He pointed her out.

"Stannis still her bosun?"

Not risking another nod, Jesamiah confirmed that he was.

"Nasty piece of work that one. I'd as soon shoot him as serve with him."

Not making a comment that could land him in trouble, Jesamiah answered, tactfully, "You know him, then, sir?"

The man indicated a scar on his face. "The two of us had a serious falling-out a few years back."

The dizziness clearing, Jesamiah took a deep breath and was grateful that the man made a grab for him as he again tottered precariously. He attempted a jest, "I'm not sure if it's the wound, or not finding my land-legs yet. The ground's pitching as much as the deck did."

"Ah, you'll soon adjust, son. Your pa always takes a few hours to do so."

That cleared Jesamiah's head as efficiently as a dousing with a bucket of cold seawater. "My pa?"

The man carefully studied the boats at anchor in the harbour through crinkled eyes. "Aye. I take it Charles is not here? No sign of his vessel out there. Has he sent you off to sea?" The man chuckled. "'Bout time, if you ask me."

Unexpected tears swam in Jesamiah's eyes. He rapidly blinked them aside. "My father died a few months ago. A week after my mother. The same sickness took them both."

The man removed his hat, wiped his hand across his mouth and nose, sniffed loudly and blinked as rapidly as Jesamiah had done. "I'm sorry to hear that, lad. Right sorry. He was a good man. She were a good woman."

Taking a step backwards, the man held out his hand. "You are, of course, Jesamiah? You are the image of Charles. Got your ma's dark Spanish eyes and hair, though."

Initially tentative, Jesamiah hesitated, but took the proffered hand and gripped it in a firm handshake. "My apologies, but you are...?"

"Taylor. Captain Malachias Taylor of the *Mermaid*, yonder." Taylor pointed to the brig.

The hint of suspicion vanishing, Jesamiah pumped Taylor's hand with joyful vigour, explaining further. "Halyard Calpin told me I would find you here. *Anna*'s not put in at Port Royal afore now. I've been hoping to meet you for weeks!"

"Old Halyard, eh?" Taylor chuckled to himself. "We go back a long way, further even than me an' your father. If he recommends you, that's good enough by me, although being your father's lad is all the testament I need. You'll do better in my crew than suffering Stannis's rough temper. However, that's to discuss later. If he is not too drunk, we'd best get Peterson to take a look at that cut. You'll be sporting a nice scar there, I reckon, even if he does, by some miracle, make a good job of putting in a few straight stitches."

"Peterson?"

"My ship's surgeon. Mind, he kills more men than he cures!" Taylor hastily grasped Jesamiah's arm, as taking a step forward, he tottered unsteadily.

"Come on, let's get you to a tavern where there's something steady to sit your backside on – and something solid inside your belly afore you topple off this quay into the harbour. Your pa would not be pleased if I let you drown within a few minutes of finally meeting up with you."

14

A generous tot of brandy and a stout wooden bench steadied Jesamiah's queasiness; another glass of the liquor masked the discomfort of Peterson inserting three ragged stitches to his forehead, the surgeon's rum-soaked breath acting as an additional anaesthetic. With the wooziness dissipating, Jesamiah took stock of his new companions; apparently congenial men, most of whose names he had instantly forgotten, except for Taylor and Peterson, the latter of whom, once his medical equipment had been thrust back into a bloodstained carpet bag, had settled into one of the Weigh Anchor's corner seats and fallen instantly asleep, a fact attested to by several loud, stentorian snores. Taylor had skimmed through the names of the men, explaining that these were his regular crew: quartermaster, cook, bosun, first mate and so on. Jesamiah could only clearly recall the quartermaster because of his unusual name. Knucklebone Jake.

The rowdiness increased as the drink liberally flowed: beer, ale, rum, Dutch Genever, Portuguese port. Although the space within the crowded tavern was distinctly limited, the *Mermaid*'s bosun, John Cleyver, was dancing a lively jig with two of the ship's sailors – Tab and Hench, Jesamiah thought their names were. Hench overdid the enthusiasm, collided with a serving wench and tumbled into a heap with her squealing and giggling

45

beneath him. Rummaging into her well-filled bodice, he made no effort to disentangle himself.

His bladder near to bursting, tears of laughter skimming his cheeks, Jesamiah made his unsteady way out into the coolness of the night air and headed for the latrine buckets arrayed in an alley alongside the tavern. Urine was prized by the nearby laundry-house for bleaching linen. The almost brim-full buckets stank, but then so did most of Port Royal. Finished, more comfortable, Jesamiah buttoned his breeches and with the tavern's raucous music loud in his ears, capered a couple of steps of the jig for himself.

He stopped, puzzled. Had they ceased playing that screeching fiddle? The off-key singing? Where a moment before the sounds had clearly carried, all was now silent apart from a mild rushing like the keening of a distant wind. Was that another voice singing? A woman? He walked to the far end of the alley and came out onto the harbourside quay. A dozen ships rested at anchor, their stern lights bobbing with the push of a slight breeze, the reflections flickering in the swell of the tide and the accumulated debris of flotsam and jetsam. He looked up at the stars; gave them a brief nod. He had been born under these patterns; on a beach in England, or so his mother had told him. Heavy with child, stumbling through the rough surf and the pains of birthing, she had fallen, injured her ankle. Was alone and frightened, but a black haired, gentle spoken woman had appeared from nowhere. A woman with a red cloak and green skirt, most assuredly Saint Anna, healer and midwife. Jesamiah had always dismissed the tale as a woman's fancy.

Another thought: were the stars the same there, in England? He kicked a stone into the water. What was he doing standing here in the dark thinking about the stars? There were two hours of his birthday left – he ought to be celebrating! He turned, eager to rejoin his new friends, but then stood, rooted to the spot. Had he taken a wrong turn? The Weigh Anchor, with another ramshackle tavern next to it, should have been straight ahead. Instead, grand two- and three-storeyed brick-built merchant stores lined either side of a well-kept street; some had a fourth attic floor beneath gabled, shingle-tiled roofs. Smoke puffed from sturdy chimneystacks. Wooden walkways fronted glazed windows, some revealing the glow of candle and lantern light behind the slatted, red, green and blue painted shutters.

The church clock struck the hour of ten. Jesamiah swivelled to look at the steeple standing high atop its whitewashed tower. He felt hairs rise on the back of his neck, his skin crawl cold. There had been no such steeple, tower or church when *Anna* had dropped anchor. None of these buildings had existed, not one of them.

Then he heard the singing again and swung around sharply, his hand going to the dagger-sheath attached to his belt. She was sitting on the quay, her legs, hidden by shadow, dangling over the edge, her tumble of waist-length golden hair flowing over her shoulders. She had her back to him, sat staring out across the black water as she sang a sad, haunting song of lost love and drowned hope; a song so beautiful he felt his heart ache and tears of longing prick at his eyes.

She must have sensed his presence, for she turned her head, her sapphire-blue eyes staring into his. She stopped singing. A smile spread over her face.

~ *You have come back to me!* ~ she said, the quiet words sounding inside his head.

"No, I..."

Her smile widened.

~ *I have been waiting so long for you to come back.* ~ She stretched out her arm, palm uppermost, and beckoned him towards her. Her curtain of hair swung aside; she was naked, her rounded breasts as white as alabaster, firm and enticing.

~ *Come, make love to me!* ~

Entranced, Jesamiah took a step nearer. She was the most beautiful creature he had ever seen.

~ *Keep away from her, son. Step aside.* ~

Jesamiah swung around. Did that hiss of responding anger come from his lips or hers? No one was there! He turned back to the girl, caught sight of her sliding from the quayside into the sea. Fearing she had fallen, he darted forward, peered anxiously into the dark water, but all he saw was the shimmer of a large, silver, fish's tail.

~ Son, trust me, she is not for you. ~

That voice. His father? How could that be?

Jesamiah squinted into the shadows cast by the buildings. "Who are you? Where are you?"

~ Heed him; he knows what you do not. ~ A different voice, female, young, gentle, with an accent he partially recognised. Where had he heard it before?

As if he were a hound questing for an elusive scent, Jesamiah peered into the darkness, swinging his head from left to right and back again. Thought, for the merest heartbeat, that he glimpsed a black-haired young girl sitting atop a pile of sweet-smelling hay.

"Who are you?" he asked again, bewildered. Was he drunk beyond reason, perhaps?

Light flooded the alley to his left as a door opened, and Knucklebone Jake stepped out from the Weigh Anchor, the sound of his urinating against the wooden wall and a loud fart not quite drowned by the raucous laughter from within.

"Ho! Jesamiah, there you are!" he called. "We thought we'd lost you, lad!"

Jesamiah shook his head. "No, sir, I'm just sampling some fresh air."

Escorting him inside, Jake chuckled. "Fresh air? Damn that, we get enough of it at sea to addle a man's senses! But you need be careful out there, boy, where the land meets the sea. You never know what mischief might be lurking , hidden within the shadows!"

15

The smoke from pipes, candles and lanterns hanging below the low-beamed rafters was akin to a thick sea-fog. Men's faces were distorted into grotesque masks by the flickering light, only their voices and laughter betraying that these were humans, not gargoyle-featured monsters. Jesamiah resumed his seat on the bench next to Taylor, the man himself narrowing his brows into a deep V.

"You alright, son? Looks like you've seen a ghost, you're as pale as a virgin's tit."

"I'm fine," Jesamiah lied, forcing a smile. He pointed to his half-filled tankard of ale. "I'm not over-used to drink."

A ghost? Had he heard, spoken to, a ghost? His father was dead. Jesamiah had sat beside him as the last breath had sighed from his body. Had seen him wrapped in a linen shroud, placed in a coffin and buried. And that young girl's accent – it was Cornish, like Mayor Smallwood's lilting burr. But why was he hearing a girl in his head? More to the point, that other woman, she had been a…He shook his head. No, there were no such things as mermaids. Or ghosts. Or voices in your head. Only the fact of too much to drink.

He lifted his tankard in a saluted toast, declared: "To the ghosts of the past!"

"To the ghosts!" Taylor repeated, swigging down his own ale.

A lengthy, broad, shadow fell over the table, the laughter in this particular corner of the tavern wavering to a ragged halt. "You ought think more of the present, Acorne, an' the consequences of forgettin' it."

"I don't recall invitin' you to join us, Stannis," Taylor drawled, his stern, disapproving gaze peering over the top of his tankard.

"An' I weren't addressin' you, Taylor, I were talkin' to the shitty boy 'ere."

Taylor set the tankard down, waved his hand in a dismissive gesture. "The boy's of my crew now, so be off with you."

Stannis ignored the remark, and the gesture. "You be a troublemaker, Acorne. Just like y' father afore you."

"How do you know who my father was?" Jesamiah retorted. "I have never mentioned him."

Stannis snorted. "I've got eyes. You be the image of Charles Mereno, even down to 'ow you walk an' talk. An' you're sitting 'ere 'obnobbin' with 'is best mate? Don't take much confirmin', do it?"

"My name is Acorne. Not Mereno."

"I don't care a bugger what y'call yourself, all I care fer is discipline aboard m' ship. An' you jumping crew ain't discipline. For m'self I don't give a tinker's cock, but Cap'n Parker's taken a shine to you, though 'e don't know your father were a whoreson pirate, who'd 'ave 'anged 'ere in Port Royal 'ad 'e not arse-licked Morgan so often."

Jesamiah's grip on his tankard tightened, the distasteful insults striking home.

Taylor rested a hand on Jesamiah's arm, murmured, "Leave it, lad. Stannis excels at being a gore-bellied boar-pig."

"We all know 'ow much Mereno paid the Spanish to take the bitch who grunted you in an' out of 'er belly off their 'ands," Stannis continued. "Your pa bragged about it in this very spot, in the tavern that used to sit 'ere, aye, an' while 'e 'ad a whore straddling his full cock as 'e did so." Stannis leered, leant forward a little. "That were a few weeks afore the quake. I remember it 'cause the whore were m'wife. The quake saved me killin' 'er fer it, an' I would 'ave killed 'im too, but coward that 'e was, 'e cleared off an' never came back. Got 'is prick rubbed by the Spanish whore instead, I reckon."

Several insults too many.

Jesamiah set his tankard down, slowly raised his gaze and looked, unblinking, into Stannis's weasel-small eyes.

"I would rather know an honourable man like Captain Parker than spit on a maggot-pie like you. I grant my father was base-born – he never made a secret of it, though, from what I know, his lady mother was a good woman. Nor was my father a pirate. He was a buccaneer who served his king fighting the Spanish." Jesamiah took a deep breath, his nostrils flaring as he leant across the table, palms flat on its wooden surface. "And my mother was not a whore."

Stannis roared laughter. "Aye," he spluttered through guffaws, "that be what she told you! She were a Spanish bitch – Mereno plucked 'er, fucked 'er, then left 'er and the result of a swollen belly to rot in that Virginian backwater."

The last stung all the more, for it was true. Charles Mereno had rarely been at home, and Jesamiah was worldly-wise enough to know it was unlikely that his father had stayed celibate through all those months away.

With dignity, though, he rose to his feet, looked at Tom Markham, sitting at the adjoining table, said, "I would thank you, Tom, if you would fetch my chest from *Anna*. I'll be wanting to take it aboard *Mermaid*, but more immediate, I'll be needing my pistol and shot from within." He stared, unblinking, at Stannis. "I assume you have a pistol and are sober enough to use it?"

Stannis laughed louder. "You threatening to attempt t'shoot me, boy? I'd like t'see you bleedin' try!"

Again, Taylor, also on his feet, urged caution.

"Jesamiah, this toad-croaker ain't worth the trouble."

Shaking off Taylor's restraining hand, Jesamiah spoke directly to Stannis, his words driven by anger, but spoken low, even and calm.

"I ain't threatening, attempting, or trying, Cap'n Taylor. This pox-raked, cock-shrivelled, braggart can meet me on the quay in half of an hour, or not, as he chooses. There is enough torchlight out there for our purpose. Unless it is you who are the coward, Stannis, not my father?"

16

———

A sizeable group of interested onlookers had gathered – word had spread that a fool-headed boy was going to be shot dead at midnight. There were few who would not support Jesamiah, for Stannis was a known bastard, and more men than could be easily counted would be only too happy to see his end. But Stannis was also vicious, and a good shot.

"Maybe he won't come?" Markham said, setting Jesamiah's wooden seaman's chest down on the quay beside his own, which he had also fetched from *Anna*. Taylor had offered him a place in *Mermaid*'s crew, an offer Tom had eagerly accepted when Taylor had added, "You could end up richer privateering with me. With the turn of the tide we'll be off after that Spaniard you encountered. I've an itch that tells me she might be carrying a few chests of treasure."

"He will come," Taylor responded from where he sat atop a barrel watching as Jesamiah opened the chest and brought out the pistol, powder and shot that Calpin had given him. "Stannis has too much swagger to stay away," he added, spitting a gob of chewed tobacco into the black sea behind his perch. "He and your pa hated each other's guts."

"I take after my father for something, then," Jesamiah answered while loading the pistol.

Taylor laughed as he reached forward to pat Jesamiah's shoulder. "You are the image of him, lad. You're handsome

53

enough to soon be taking after your pa where the women are concerned as well, I reckon!"

Crimson flushed Jesamiah's face. He had not yet discovered the delights of the female sex, a fact that was beginning to become slightly embarrassing.

Noticing, Taylor guffawed louder, and then sobered rapidly as Stannis, accompanied by two of his stalwart cronies, strode onto the quay. Taylor slid from the barrel and sauntered in front of Jesamiah to form a protective stance.

"I am not keen on losing any of my crew," he said, folding his arms. "What say you, Stannis, to a handshake and we forget this nonsense?"

Stannis removed his hat, flicked an imagined speck of dust from the crown and replaced it. "I don't give a gnat's fart about your crew, Taylor. If the squit in question thinks it's too dark to shoot straight, I'll accommodate killin' 'im at dawn."

Jesamiah clicked the hammer to half-cock and politely, but firmly, pushed Malachias Taylor aside. "There's more than enough light for me to see your fat lardy-bulk, Stannis."

"You do both know that Good Queen Bess, may she rest in peace, made duelling an offence back in fifteen hundred-and-something?" Tom Markham stated, ushering a few overeager onlookers to stand back.

"Did she now?" Jesamiah answered, stepping forward to take up position, his pistol by his thigh, pointing downward. "Pity she's not here to remind us of it, then, isn't it? Is this far enough of a distance, Stannis? Or do you wish to move forward a pace or two to see better?"

Stannis grunted, made no reply. Two pistols dangled from ribbons suspended around his neck; he untied one, inspected the weapon to ensure it was correctly primed and loaded, sniffed disdainfully, and shifting his stance so that he stood at an angle to Jesamiah, raised the weapon.

"I'll take that as a yes, then," Jesamiah said, also moving to imitate his opponent's pose.

"On my count of three, you may both fire," Taylor said, ensuring he stood well back. Several other onlookers took his cue and shuffled aside. "Cock your weapons."

With his thumb, Stannis clicked the hammer home, pointed the pistol straight at Jesamiah's heart.

Jesamiah raised his own weapon.

"One," Taylor counted.

Jesamiah clicked his pistol hammer home.

"Two."

There came a loud splash from the water below the quay; distracted, frowning, Jesamiah turned his head towards the sound and was sure, in that split fraction of a heartbeat, that he saw the silver sparkle of a fish's tail. A sparkle that was dimmed by the flash of gunpowder and the flare of flame and smoke as Stannis fired.

Jesamiah staggered, fell. Uproar! Shouting disapproval, the crowd surged forward, some to gather around Jesamiah, others to jostle Stannis.

Taylor shoved the men aside, his face like thunder, his fists raised. "I hadn't counted! I hadn't said three! You bloody murderer! You coward cockroach, you—"

"It's alright!" Jesamiah shouted, scrabbling to his feet, Tom Markham and a few others helping him up. "I'm alright, he grazed my arm, that's all!"

He pushed his way through the crowd, his own expression as murderous as Taylor's, barely feeling the ooze of blood dribbling down his skin beneath the torn shirt and coat. "I'm alright," he repeated, shouting to be heard.

The clamour of outrage quietened a little. He halted two yards from Stannis, men parting so that the two opponents had a clear view of each other. A hush fell – only a few murmured whispers, a shuffling of feet, someone coughed; the slap of the tide against the wooden pillars supporting the quay.

Quietly, Jesamiah said, "I still have my shot to make."

As if Port Royal's militia had suddenly appeared, the crowd hurriedly moved aside. In the cleared space, Jesamiah strode forward, his pistol still to hand, the trickle of blood reaching his wrist. He stood, one pace in front of Stannis, face-to-face, eye-to-eye, their breath intermingling, the smell of their sweat rank on their bodies. Jesamiah uncocked his pistol, transferred it to his left hand, and with his bloodied right, tugged at the ribbon holding Stannis's second weapon. The knot unfastened, and the pistol clattered to the wooden planks beneath their feet. Jesamiah kicked the gun aside, heard it plop into the water. He glanced at the length of royal-blue ribbon, and smiling, claimed it for himself by shoving it into his coat pocket.

"I'll be keeping it," he said, "as a reminder that for men like you, honour can be as fragile as a skein of summer mist." He wiped the trail of blood from his skin onto Stannis's shirt, then transferred the pistol back to his right hand. Reaching up with his left, removed Stannis's fancy hat, its elaborate feather somewhat damp and bedraggled in the cool night air. "I'll be taking this too," Jesamiah said as he turned and strode ten paces, then swivelling on his heel, turned back again.

Stannis had turned pale. As with all bullies, beneath the crude words, beating fists and kicking feet, he was nothing but a sham when confronted by a taste of his own medicine.

"You wouldn't dare shoot me, boy!" he taunted, "not in cold blood. You 'aven't the guts, the balls, or the ability."

"My father," Jesamiah said, "would have been able to put a bullet dead centre between your eyes."

"But you ain't your ragbag of a father are you?" Stannis crowed. "You've said so y'self!"

To the disappointment of the crowd, and an accompanying groan of partial contempt, Jesamiah nodded. "You are quite right, I am not," he said, and started to stride away – then stopped, and spinning around, tossed the hat high into the night air. It hung there a moment, a dark patch against the silver stars, then as it began to fall Jesamiah raised the pistol, aimed and fired.

The hat landed almost at Stannis's feet, but Taylor was the one who picked it up and inspecting it, poked his index finger through a scorched, bullet-sized hole.

"My father," Jesamiah stated as he tucked the pistol through his belt, then went to his seaman's chest and hefted it onto his shoulder, "was, in my opinion, about as good at being a father as is a piss pot made of paper. I want nothing to do with him, nor do I want to remember him, emulate him or use his name." He walked to the end of the quay, handed the chest down to one of the crew from the *Mermaid* waiting in the moored longboat, and said over his shoulder, "But I am grateful to him for teaching me how to shoot a pistol as accurately as he could."

He straightened, hands on his hips; stared, frowning, at Malachias Taylor. "Are we going to catch this tide? Or are we to stand here gawping until sunrise?"

All he wanted to do was get aboard *Mermaid* and hope that not one single soul was noticing that his hands and legs were shaking, that his bladder was about to void itself and he was fighting hard not to vomit all over his boots.

17

CORNWALL, ENGLAND

The Reverend Garrick was not in a congenial mood. Which was not unusual when the weekly composition of his lengthy Sunday sermon was not going to his liking. He had been called away that mid-morning to spiritually attend a sick man, one of the village's poorer fishermen. The rain had soaked through his clothing, and on reaching the cottage – hovel, more like – he found the wretched man to be already dead. A fact he considered to be most inconsiderate of the man himself, and his newly-made widow.

"A wasted journey," he grumbled yet again, as his wife began to clear away the remains of the family's frugal bread, cheese and ale supper. The Reverend could well afford better fare, but considered extra expense to be gluttony and therefore unnecessary.

"These people have no respect for their betters," he complained, frowning as his wife made no response to her husband's comment, but handed the last piece of bread, spread with home-churned butter, to the youngest of her surviving brood, her daughter.

The girl, Tiola, thanked her mother, but tore the chunk in half to share it with her next-eldest brother, eleven-year-old Bennett, three years her senior. She should have kept her attention on the bread, instead, she said, "Would it not have been better for them to have summoned old Agnes Pollock? Her knowledge of herbs and potions might have been more useful than prayers and sermons."

Within five minutes, the girl found her face to be red and stinging from the harsh blow her father had dealt, her mouth foul from the taste of salt water, administered to cleanse her tongue of blasphemy, and the door to her small attic chamber bolted, with the promise that it would not be unlocked until she mended her ungodly ways.

She did not mind her room, nor the prospect of several days of solitude – anything that meant she could avoid her father was always a boon. She had a window through which, when the shutter was thrown wide, she could gaze out across the cliffs to the sea, and wonder where the boy with the black hair was now, what he was doing, who he was with. She had these, and other, thoughts for company, and was well used to being confined to her room, welcomed it as an escape, not as a punishment.

Outside, the rain had turned to snow. Tiola snuggled into her bed, warmed by woollen blankets and a goose-down quilt, listening to the raised voice of her father seeping up from the kitchen two floors below. His words were always spoken loud, the volume increasing with righteous indignity. In church of a Sunday morning, none in the congregation ever dozed during his delivered sermons.

She knew that she was right about Agnes, but knew, also, that she should not have spoken aloud. The vehement statement of, '*It is time an end was put to the devil's witch!*' reached her ears, followed soon after by a crash of the front door as it slammed shut.

Wrapping the quilt around her shoulders, Tiola went to the window, watched as her father walked with long, purposeful strides, towards the village, his boots leaving dark prints in the settling snow. Heard, an hour later, the blood-stirred shouts of men, saw the bobbing lights of many smoke-streaming tar torches, and then the blaze of a fire up on the cliff height, a cloud of red, orange, yellow and black smoke drifted against the white flutters of snow.

There had been screams too, drifting on the wind, an old

woman's pleas for mercy. Mercy? The Reverend Garrick had no sense of the word, nor did the villagers when their blood was stirred by the false claims of a man who was the mainstay of the area and who they looked up to and respected. For all that the respect was mistakenly given. Nor was there respect for the law, not when the nearest judge was more than twenty miles away in Truro, nor when the old ways and beliefs of doing things persisted in the minds of bigoted people.

As she watched the fire on the clifftop, tears filled Tiola's eyes. Witches, men like her father insisted, were the devil's whores, and the only way to cleanse a possessed soul was by the heat of fire. But an old woman, with wrinkled, brown-marked skin, who muttered to herself, who lived on her own with a cat for company and a goat for milk, who had knowledge of healing and herbs was not a witch, just an old woman.

Witches kept themselves hidden, for they were the Wise Ones of Light who healed and cared, not killed or maimed. The Craft of the White Witch was passed, in secret, from grandmother to granddaughter, and although her Gift was not yet full awoken, Tiola did not need the Sight to know that it was not old Agnes who was the witch, but herself.

18

AT SEA. DECEMBER 5TH 1708

Aboard *Mermaid*, Jesamiah trudged barefoot in his old sailor's clothes around and around the capstan with the other men. Each circuit laboriously winching in the heavy anchor cable, feeding its great length inward to be neatly stowed on the raised slats down in the bilge. Its sodden weight stank, and weed, crabs and limpets clung to it. Kennet, the ship's cook, gleefully picked off everything that was suitable – or even unsuitable – for his copper stewpot.

The familiar, rhythmical task had steadied Jesamiah's reaction of fear, giving him time to think. That clammy weight, like an undigested helping of stodgy porridge in his stomach, had taken him by surprise. Time and again, when Phillipe had been overzealous with his bullying, Jesamiah had thought he was going to die – on more than one occasion had even wished it in order to put an end to the pain and humiliations. Facing Stannis and that raised pistol had not hit home until he had stowed his own weapon away. He could have been killed. Wounded. That had frightened him more. Once you were dead, that was an end to it, but the pain of a wound, the loss of an arm, a leg, sight?

He shivered, and put his back into pushing the capstan those last few turns. *Clunk, clunk, clunk*, it moved more slowly; the hull was pulling heavily on the anchor cable, the men bent

61

almost double as they tramped around and around, their bare feet slapping in rhythm: *clunk, stamp, clunk, stamp, clunk…*

Jesamiah glanced at the shore. Flaring torches were set along the harbour wall, lantern-glow spilled from the open doors of taverns; starlight rippled across the surface of the restless sea. He could so easily have been lying dead over there! He turned his attention to the topmen at the masthead, as agile as cats, running out along the yards to drop to the footropes below.

"Standby on capstan," someone called.

"Loose heads'ls!" A command from Taylor, and almost immediately the answering flap and clatter of released canvas.

"Hands aloft! Loose tops'ls…Man the braces – look lively there you men!"

Men were dashing about on the vibrating yards, utterly indifferent to the height above the deck. The main and fore topsails billowed outward like the bowed shape of a soldier's breastplate, then sank almost flat, billowed again, the sound cracking and banging.

"Anchor's aweigh!" the shout came, and the untethered brig suddenly swung across the steep troughs of the bay, the men falling and slithering at the braces as they fought to haul the great yards round to catch the truculent wind.

"Lee braces. Heave away."

Mermaid, enjoying her freedom, plunged faster and faster astride the wind. At the capstan, men ceased their toil, leaning on the wooden bars, panting heavily and catching their breath, Jesamiah among them.

With a roar like thunder, the topsails filled and hardened. *Mermaid* canted further over, white water gushing above the rail and sluicing along the deck. The running water and the sea creaming past her hull, the gurgling and churning mixing with the singing wind, the creaking of wood, the slapping of rope and the thrumming of the rigging.

Jesamiah eased his aching back, and rubbed at the bullet-scratch on his arm. He winced at the throbbing from the stitches in his head. Taylor called another series of orders; men ran to haul on ropes and the gaff rose towards the night sky, its blocks and tackles squeaking in protest. *Mermaid* settled into her course, thrusting into the first roller beyond the protection of the harbour as if she were the creature she was named for; ploughed onward, delighted to be where she belonged, running before the wind and heading towards the open ocean.

Frank O'Bartlett, a short man in his mid-forties with a face as brown and wrinkled as a walnut, stood at the helm, his hands gentling the spokes as he eased *Mermaid* into the wind, his intense gaze on the edge of the mainsail for that slight shiver to tell him he had her tamed to his satisfaction.

Jesamiah, his work for a moment done, watched him, admiring his skill, studying how his touch was light, but firm.

"You gentle a vessel," O'Bartlett said, Jesamiah noticing a hint of Irish in his accent. "Never bully her, see, or she'll buck agin ye, and refuse t'do ye biddin'. Women an' ships alike prefer t'be gentled by a man, not bullied."

Again, Jesamiah felt his face redden. Maybe the time was approaching when he needed to sort this recurring 'sex' situation? That would have to wait until the next landfall, however. There were no women, apart from that bare-breasted carved figurehead, aboard *Mermaid*.

"Men and boys, too," he said to hide that awkward moment of embarrassed silence. "Bullying is not right for anyone to endure."

"I'll agree wi' ye there," O'Bartlett said.

Tom Markham was at the rail, talking to Taylor. Seeing Jesamiah, the Captain beckoned him to join them.

"We've been discussing that Spaniard," he said, jabbing his finger towards an indiscriminate point far out to sea. "Tom agrees she could be heavy-laden, heading home for Cádiz. What say you?"

Jesamiah scratched at his chin. A prickle of whiskers were starting to sprout, and he would soon have to consider shaving as well as think on what to do about women. He fiddled with the acorn earring dangling from his right lobe, twiddled the length of his trophy, the blue ribbon that he had braided into his hair. All of it playing for time while he considered an answer.

"She was certainly low in the water, and I am not totally convinced that the captain fell for my performance. My Spanish was sound enough, but did I look like a merchant's master? I think he realised we were small fry, not worth bothering with."

"Tom thinks the same," Taylor confirmed, "and I think it would be worth *our* while to see if we can catch up with her."

Tom Markham stared out into the starlit darkness at the frothing white surge of water in *Mermaid*'s wake. "She's a damn sight bigger than us. More guns. More men."

Taylor slapped him on the shoulder, laughed. "Aye, but is she as fast and manoeuvrable as we are?" He paused, laughed again, louder, added, "Only one way to find out!"

He walked off, chuckling, heading for the privacy of his cabin; shouting as he went for men to tidy away some trailing cordage.

19

Jesamiah leant his arms on the taffrail, taking in satisfying breaths of sea and night air. The faint lights and silhouetted buildings of Port Royal were rapidly diminishing. He was glad to see the back of the place, if truth be told. There were too many echoes of his father there.

"You must have known Stannis well, then?" he asked Tom, who had pulled his clay pipe from a pocket and lit it, sheltering his tinderbox beneath the protection of the gunwale. As with most ships, smoking was permitted on the open deck, but, for fear of fire, never below.

"Not really," he answered at length. "He's a good ten years older than am I, and he were a man grown before the quake hit. I remember his roughness, though, and his constant arguing and shouting. His folks were equally rough. They owned the tavern that stood where the Weigh Anchor does now. Made a fortune, did that place, aye, an' we're not talking about the ale-sellin' neither."

Jesamiah frowned, waited for further explanation.

"That what Stannis taunted you with? Your pa messin' around with his wife? It were true – well, I reckon it were," he said between puffing energetically at his pipe to keep it drawing. "She'd been with nearly every other sailor in Port Royal, no reason t'believe Cap'n Mereno was an exception."

Seeing Jesamiah's frown deepen, Tom chuckled. "The tavern

was also a brothel. Stannis married their best asset when he were eighteen, aye, and kept the money from her earnings for himself. She were killed outright when the quake struck." Tom abandoned the surly pipe, knocked the ash out over the side. "They found her and her client beneath the rubble, still...how shall we say? 'Conjoined'?" He laughed aloud. "The earth certainly moved for the poor bugger payin' her that afternoon!"

"Was my father at Port Royal often?" Jesamiah asked after a short while.

"Aye, and him I do remember, though partly from listening to my pa and others. Your father was highly respected – him, Henry Jennings, Taylor and Morgan. It was your father who tried to persuade Morgan to take it easy on the drink, but even with that and his uncommon temper, Morgan was loved in Port Royal. 'Specially by the women, although he had little time for them. His love was for the sea and Spanish gold." Tom sniffed and wiped his hand across his mouth. "Word was that he preferred young boys or men in his bed. No proof, o' course," he added hastily.

Jesamiah asked sharply, not daring to believe such a slander, "Are you hinting that my father was Morgan's lover?"

Tom raised his arms in defence. "Nay, your pa and Jennings – he were about your age back then – enjoyed their women too much to waste time with a fat-rump like Morgan."

Tactfully, he kept quiet about the tales of what had gone on when the three of them had sailed in pursuit of the Spanish. Nor did such rumours fit well with Morgan and Mereno falling out over a blonde beauty who lured men to the starlit beach to seduce them.

"So the story goes, Morgan got angry with a lass and beat her to within an inch of her life. Your pa saved her. He went for Morgan. Bare fists, hit him hard. He never would stand men abusing women, your pa. As a result, Morgan ordered him to leave Port Royal and never come back. If he did, he'd hang him." Tom leant further across the rail, staring at the frothing sea. "Soon after, Morgan died. Cut your pa up something terrible, that did." A sudden thought came to Tom: what if Morgan had attacked the girl because he had been angry with

Mereno for spreading his affections elsewhere? One jealous lover against another? He kept the suspicion to himself.

They were both silent a moment, then Jesamiah asked what had become of the girl.

"Ah," Tom answered, somewhat brighter of spirit, "she were never seen again. Several stories emerged, of course, some that your pa killed her for causing the rift between himself and Morgan – unlikely, for as I said, he would not abuse women. Others said that she sailed off with him, found a life elsewhere. Some claimed that she drowned herself and the Sea Goddess, Tethys, turned her into a mermaid. Some even say that she were a mermaid all along."

Jesamiah stayed quiet, picturing in his mind that beauty he had seen; her breasts, her bare legs dangling into the water...

Markham indicated that he had to return to work, and squeezed Jesamiah's arm. "Your pa loved your ma, rest assured of that. He was a good man, and you have the makings of being one yourself – as long as you don't go challenging too many men like Stannis to duels." He winked and hurried off. It did no harm to lie to the boy. He need not know about his father's fondness for sex, although he would probably work it out for himself one day.

Port Royal was barely visible now, but Jesamiah could not shake the vision of what he had seen from the corner of his eye as he had stamped around the capstan. The town as it was before the earthquake reduced it to rubble, and the blonde kneeling at the edge of the surf. Was she a mermaid? Jesamiah sighed, signalled that he was coming when someone shouted his name. Perhaps it was the salt in the sea air that brought on such fanciful ideas?

20

———

Halfway through the next morning, Taylor passed word for Jesamiah to attend him in his Great Cabin. Nervously, Jesamiah scurried aft from the beakhead, worrying that he had done something wrong.

"Cap'n? You wanted to see me?"

Taylor was sitting at a beech-wood table pushed to one side of the cabin. For special occasions it would be brought out to the centre, its side-flaps opened and set with a, somewhat yellowed by age, linen tablecloth, silver knives, forks, spoons, and a chipped Bristol China dinner service. The table's splendour, however, was marred by more than a few deep, jagged, scratches and the haphazard scattering of paraphernalia: charts; maps; navigational items; an inkstand. Shavings from goose-quills. Two clay pipes, both snapped in half; several empty brandy bottles. It looked like the table had not been cleared for a celebration feast in months.

"Ah, Acorne, come in. I want to talk with you about this Spaniard." Taylor walked to the door, flung it open and shouted for Kennet to bring coffee. "Let me finish writing this inventory and I'll be with you, lad."

Jesamiah nodded; he was in no particular hurry.

"Can't stomach this necessity for keeping accounts and ledgers," Taylor grumbled. "Jake's a good quartermaster when

68

it comes to finances, but not for administration. No idea why I made him quartermaster, really."

"Get someone else, then. I doubt Jake will object. He seems to be always grumbling about it."

"Aye, loud grumbles at that. He likes the position, but not the work involved. You read and write, don't you? Know your figures? Additions and subtractions?"

For a moment, Jesamiah was tempted to say that he did not – he was more than happy with his simple duties. But pride got the better of hesitation. "That I do. And the understanding of navigation." Then he added, with a reluctant mumble, "Pa taught me."

Taylor jabbed his index finger into Jesamiah's shoulder, emphasising his point. "See, your pa did care for ye. He'd not have bothered 'else." Chuckling, he rummaged through several papers looking for a particular bill of sale.

"You reckon you could sort this mess out?" he asked after failing to find it. "Keep everything in order?"

There! Jesamiah knew he should have kept his mouth shut. "I reckon I could."

"Right, then." Taylor picked up a quill, dipped it into the inkpot and began to scribble. "I'll let Knucklebone Jake know that I've made you quartermaster's clerk. Jake'll expect you to do all the tedious accounts, of course."

"But," Jesamiah protested, "I very much enjoy working aloft with the sails."

"You'll still be doin' that. Maybe I'll promote you to head topman one day."

"Will I get paid extra?"

"As topman? Aye. Quartermaster's clerk, nay. You'll stay at the same share of any profit we make for the total of one year, then, providing you show you are capable I will raise that by one quarter-share, which becomes a full share if you replace Jake at some point in the future, or I offer you a different position of similar authority." He held out his hand. "Deal?"

Tempted to haggle over payment, Jesamiah thought better of that aspect, but offered, "Four months."

"Six."

"Done." Jesamiah grinned and they shook on it.

"Good. You start tomorrow, after I have informed Jake of his good fortune. Now, let me get this damned task completed."

Jesamiah wandered round the cabin. It was not big, but had a higher ceiling than most ships and was at least three yards more in length than Captain Parker's poky cabin aboard *Anna*. But then, *Anna* was a merchant ship. Every spare inch of space was essential to store cargo.

To one side of the range of salt-grimed stern windows stood a magnificent wooden figurehead of a seaman. It must have weighed a great deal, for it was elm and filled the space from floor to ceiling – almost six feet, with the decking below reinforced to take the weight. Jesamiah stood admiring it. The top half of the head, from eyebrows up, was missing, but skilfully carved dark locks billowed about the clean-shaven face as if blown by a tempestuous wind. Beneath the chin, a froth of carved lace poked from a scarlet-painted coat with silver buttons. In its right hand, a pistol – a real one, although, judging by the accumulated rust and dirt, it would never fire.

"Handsome, isn't he?" Taylor said at Jesamiah's shoulder.

Jesamiah spun round, stifling a gasp. He hated people coming up behind him, a legacy of Phillipe's doing.

Not noticing, Taylor continued, "Your pa found him floating face down near the coast of Brazil, oh, years back now. I reckon he's adorned the cabin of every ship your pa commanded."

"So, why is it here?" Jesamiah asked.

"What? Aboard *Mermaid*?" Taylor laughed, a deep-throated chuckle. "Lord bless you, son, *Mermaid* was always your pa's before he upgraded to that fine ship of his, *La Sorenta*. I was his quartermaster for..." he paused, scratched at his chin, "well, never mind for how many years. He passed her to me, made me her Captain."

Jesamiah stared again at the figurehead's face. "But he decided to leave it here, not move it?"

"There's been more than one *Mermaid*. He got fed up with shifting the bloody thing."

Examining the exquisite carving more closely, Jesamiah asked, "Who is he, then?"

"Who? No idea. Your pa had it painted like this to honour Morgan, but there's a good bit of himself in that face as well." Taylor stroked the figurehead's arm with affection. "It was in a sorry state when we found it floating – thought it were a drowned man at first, till we pulled it from the water. Riddled with worm, rotten and dented, but we had a good carpenter aboard who repaired it well enough. I can't rightly recall, but I'd hazard the fellow deliberately re-chiselled the face to resemble your pa." He looked from the figurehead to Jesamiah and back again. "Aye, you've got the same features. Eyes are different, though. Them o' yours are your lady mother's eyes, God rest her."

He went to take two steaming coffee cups from Kennet, who had entered, grumbling that he was the ship's esteemed cook, not a coffee-house keeper.

"And a fine cook you are, my friend, but your captain also appreciates your excellent coffee," Taylor lied.

Kennet's scowl deepened and he let the wooden door bang as he left, unimpressed by the flattery.

Winking at Jesamiah, Taylor whispered, "Actually, his coffee rarely tastes like coffee, but he is the best cook we have." He pointed to a chair. "Sit yourself down and tell me all you remember about that Spaniard. It might not be useful, but, then again, it might."

21

THE CARIBBEAN SEA

It was not the Spaniard they sighted first, but a French barque. As attacks went it was unremarkable, although initially a little frightening for Jesamiah, who did not know what to expect – except that a Chase could end in your body being buried at sea. *Mermaid* had cut in across her bow, fired a single warning shot, manoeuvred to larboard and took all her victim's wind, effectively crippling her. Undermanned, underpaid, the crew had given a token resistance out of misplaced loyalty to their useless captain, but *Mermaid* was already alongside, men throwing grappling lines and securing boarding planks. Jesamiah boarded her with his companions, weapons drawn, pistols firing, all of it accompanied by blood-curdling yells, hollered shouts and the acrid stink of gun smoke. That was the point of attack: to make as much noise as possible, adding to the fear and thereby accomplishing a swift and easy result. Not a single man, on either side, had received a wound. The *Mermaid's* crew soon emptied the French hold of cargo, and looted useful items – sailcloth, cordage, timber, lamp oil and barrels of salt beef – and relieved her captain of the wine stored in his apology of a cabin, along with a box of fifty gold sovereigns.

Three days later, they found their intended quarry, moved in closer to ensure it was her, and then backed off. Taylor had outlined his plan to the crew, his old hands accepting his decision, for no matter how daft or daring, his actions usually worked – and worked well. The few new members, Tom and Jesamiah included, were more doubtful.

"Bloody madness," Tom had muttered almost non-stop for the first three hours while they languished at a discreet distance, waiting for night to fall.

It took skill, nous and luck to run a ship under full sail fast in the dark. Taylor had all three qualities – and more besides. They overhauled the Spaniard, thankful that the cloud cover was enough to obscure the moon and stars, then, as dawn peeped below the eastern horizon, Taylor ordered men aloft to furl the topgallants, the highest sails, for they would be spotted first. As was proven when Jesamiah, sitting up in the crosstrees, called down, excitedly, that he could see the Spaniard's uppermost spread of canvas. For her, there was no reason for stealth. For her, only the surprise of seeing a vessel that had apparently appeared from nowhere etched against the skyline a few miles ahead.

An hour later the Spaniard had drawn closer, within cannon range. *Mermaid* was vulnerable, for Taylor had ordered most of his crew either below or to hide beneath piles of canvas. Their sails were ill-set, spilling wind whenever they clumsily tacked to change course, the depleted crew giving the impression of rising panic.

"Fire Old Jim," Taylor called from where he stood beside O'Bartlett at the helm. "Make it a poor, very bad shot with not enough powder to sink a bucket, let alone a galleon."

Named 'Old Jim' after the first King James, the starboard bow chaser belched black smoke more than anything else, the ball lazily arcing out across the sea between the two vessels, only to plop without any semblance of a threat into a white-capped roller several hundred yards from the Spaniard.

Taylor counted to one hundred. "Fire him again, as bad as you did before." Muttered under his breath, "And Gawd help you if you ever handle a cannon like that at any other time."

A second disconsolate boom, a second pathetic shot that had no sense of threat about it.

The Spaniard answered; the ball she fired dropping in a

plume of menacing spray within four yards of *Mermaid*'s stern. Taylor smiled. So far, everything was going to plan: the Spanish had fallen for it, they assumed their prospective prize to be a poorly-manned, lubberly wastrel of a merchant. Easy pickings.

The order to 'Give this English bastard a peppering' came loud and clear across the water from the Spanish, obeyed with resounding delight as shot from their two forward swivel guns spattered *Mermaid* with little harm done. On the more northerly course, Taylor nodded to O'Bartlett, who, overemphasising his action at the helm, turned *Mermaid*'s transom towards the Spaniard as if about to attempt to make a run for it. The whoop of pleasure from the Spaniard's crew as they drove to follow her crashed across the shortening space of clear water along with another well-placed cannon shot. That confirmed it: *Mermaid* was wanted as a prize in as much of one piece as possible. Had those gunners aboard the Don wanted to do damage, *Mermaid* would be in splintered pieces by now.

Several more minutes and the pursuer's bowsprit was only a few yards behind *Mermaid*'s stern – it was now or never that the rest of Taylor's plan could be put into action. The Spaniard made ready to overhaul, the two vessels racing together as if they were hounds let loose on the hunt. The Spaniard fired a forwardmost gun as she began to draw level. With a loud crash, it struck *Mermaid* amidships, but resulted in little damage.

"Surrender!" came a voice in poor English from the Spanish quarterdeck. "Surrender and your mans will comes to not 'arm, Inglish merchant!"

Taylor walked almost insolently to the rail and stared a full four heartbeats at the Spanish captain, who stood in more or less the exact same pose.

"Like fokking hell I will," Taylor muttered. He raised his hat as if he were about to acknowledge and agree, then brought it downward fast and sharp, bellowing at the same moment, *"Now!"*

Mermaid's gun ports flew open, guns appeared from nowhere, as did dozens of armed, shouting men. O'Bartlett spun the helm, and *Mermaid*'s cannons roared in a synchronised rolling broadside, gun after gun – *boom…boom…boom…boom* –

each shot pounding into the galleon as she came alongside, *Mermaid* herself reeling from the recoil of the blasting. The iron balls sliced through the Spaniard's rail and hull, tearing everything to shreds, gouging great lengths of splinters as deadly as any conventional weapon. A direct hit on one of the guns on the galleon's poop deck!

Mermaid's crew, to the aghast watching Spanish, had suddenly trebled in number; dozens of men appearing, banging on the rail with anything to hand – their pistols, cutlasses, small bucklers that acted as miniature shields, every man yelling at the top of his voice the terrifying boarding chant of *"Death! Death! Death!"*

Mermaid's bow smashed into the Spaniard, and the *pop, pop, pop* of small arms, along with the cries of the wounded, joined the cheering as a wave of men flung themselves up and onto the Spaniard's deck.

"Go, lads!" Taylor shouted as he drew one of his pistols from the leather strap aslant his chest and jumped up atop the quarterdeck rail. As nonchalantly as if he were going from a longboat to a harbourside quay, he stepped across to the Spanish vessel's mizzen channel, grasped the shrouds, over the rail, and leapt down onto his opponent's deck. Almost within the same movement he aimed the pistol and shot the Spanish captain clean through his heart.

22

As ordered, Jesamiah had been crouched low beside the forward gunwale, shrouded by the torn canvas of an old sail. It had been hot and airless, giving only a limited view of the deck – the not knowing exactly what was happening adding to the fear building in his guts and bladder. Tom Markham had noticed his pale, green-tinged complexion.

"You alright?" he had asked, nudging Jesamiah with his elbow to gain his attention.

"I…I think so," had come the hesitant response as Jesamiah switched from fiddling with his earring to tugging at what he was hoping to regard as his lucky blue ribbon. "Although, I'm not sure my belly agrees."

Tom had laughed. "Your first *proper* fight – that Frenchie don't count, do it? You've done well in the practice bouts with Taylor, me and the other lads, but the real thing takes us all like you're feeling. You'll be fine once we get started. The blood-rush takes over."

"It's my own blood-spill I'm bothered about," Jesamiah had answered with a grimace, his right hand tightening around the pistol he was holding, his left clutching a small, round buckler.

"There's only one certainty in life, lad: death. Best to look the Grim Reaper in the eye and meet him in a fair fight. Go out screaming your lungs hoarse because you're aiming to kill him before he kills you."

It proved to be good advice.

When the signal came and the concealing canvas was thrown aside, the hidden men lurched upward in one bellowing mass. Even had he wanted to, there was no way Jesamiah could have remained behind. Lifted as a wave lifts a ship, he was swept along in the furore to pound his pistol butt and buckler on the rail, to scream and shout the death chant, to leap across to the Spaniard's deck, his throat already sore from yelling. He aimed, shot a man before a bullet finished him first. Reversed the spent pistol, sidestepped and used it like a club to fell another man running at him open-mouthed, dagger raised…He hastily tucked the pistol into his belt, drew his own dagger and slashed at another man – unaware of what he was doing, just doing it. He protected his left side with the buckler, raised it as a boarding axe slewed down towards him, his arm jarring with the impact, but it was a wrong move by the axe-wielding Spaniard. With his opponent's left side exposed, Jesamiah thrust his dagger into the man, up and under his ribs.

"*Always under and up,*" Malachias had instructed in their training fights, "*never in and down, or your blade will do little damage, merely skim across the ribs.*"

Once, he thought he heard a girl shout a warning. Had he not turned that fraction of an inch towards the sound, it would have been his throat cut by a dagger blade, not his arm.

~ *I am Tiola,* ~ he thought he heard her whisper. ~ *I am here to watch over you.* ~

Then he forgot all about her – concentrated on staying alive.

23
___

The snow had fallen slowly, but steadily, for several days, blanketing the cliffs, turning the sea a sullen slate-grey. Great drifts, driven by a mithering wind, had piled against the stone walls of the church, but the men had trudged up from the village and used shovels to cut a path to the door. Nothing would stop the Reverend from ensuring his Sunday service would take place. By nine of the morning, the sun had come out and shone with God's favour on the land, sparkling on the snow, glinting on the frozen stream and the icicles that had dripped and solidified from walls and roofs.

Tiola sat next to her mother in the front pew, her brothers to her other side, her hands thrust into a cylindrical woollen muff lined with rabbit fur, her head down, her eyes staring at the pattern of colours from the church windows cast upon the slate flag floor. Dust motes danced in the shaft of sunlight. If glory must be given to God, then was not this the way to honour Him? Through Nature's wonders?

She looked up at the window directly behind the altar, Christ In Majesty dominated, but beneath his feet, a ship rode upon white-capped blue waves. Two angels hovered either side of the single mast, their hands outstretched. In protection or warning, she wondered as she studied the scene.

As she stared, the words of her father's sermon became lost to her as a meaningless, background drone, like the sound of bees busy in a meadow on a drowsy, hot summer's day. She fancied that she could see the waves moving, the little ship lifting and dipping. There was a pale figurehead at the bow – a mermaid.

But then, through the bright, sun-dappled rainbow colours, a mist descended, a mist of billowing smoke from canon and pistol fire. She heard shouting and screams – screams of blood-lust for battle, of wounds given and received.

The boy was there – more grown now, so man, not boy. He was fighting, whether attacking or defending she could not tell. Someone was behind him, dagger raised, slashing for his throat...

~ *Beware!* ~ she shouted in her mind, smiled as the blade made no more than a glancing slice to his arm.

~ *I am Tiola,* ~ she whispered, again as thought, inside his head not spoken words.

~ *I am here to watch over you.* ~

24

Mermaid's surgeon, as always on the wrong side of sober, tipped a pungent mixture of salt water and vinegar over the gash on Jesamiah's arm, making him gasp; the treatment hurt more than the wound.

"You'll shout louder if'n you lose yer arm if it's gawn gangrene," Peterson drawled as, wiping his bloodied hands down an equally bloodied square of sacking used as an apron, he turned away from Jesamiah to tend his next patient. Several had already died despite his administrations. Glancing at their dreadful wounds, Jesamiah realised that, perhaps, they were fortunate to pass away quickly rather than endure hours, days, of indescribable pain.

"My assistant will bandage you up," the surgeon added, somewhat gruffly. "Douse the wound regularly with salt water and it might heal clean."

Jesamiah nodded. He remembered his mother using the same method to tend various scrapes and lacerations. Phillipe had caused most of them. Funny, he had not thought of his half-brother for a while. He had asked Taylor to send word to Halyard Calpin that he was serving aboard *Mermaid*, and then buried all memory of Virginia.

Up on deck, Spanish bodies had been tossed overboard, not all of them necessarily dead bodies, but no one particularly bothered with minor matters such as that. Their own dead crew had been given to the deep with reverence and a gold piece tucked into their clothing to pay for their journey to Heaven, or wherever it was their souls went.

The crew were passing around kegs of brandy that had been found in stored in the hold, and a few men could be heard shouting a slapdash inventory of the valuables they were finding in the hold. A first inspection had confirmed the Spaniard was carrying gold, silver, gems and other riches. That was all they had needed as an excuse to celebrate, the quartermaster Knucklebone Jake confirming that, after the pre-agreed percentage paid to Jamaica's Governor and the English Government, each man would be the richer by several hundred gold pieces. Although it had been Jesamiah who had rough-tallied the figures, not Jake.

"I have no idea what to do with my share," he confided to Taylor that evening.

"Most'll spend it on women, alcohol, tobacco and gambling as soon as we make harbour." Taylor pointed to where nearly everyone was sprawled, snoring off a surfeit of drink. "A few might squirrel some away, but most'll not have anything left after a few weeks."

Jesamiah pulled at his bloodstained and torn shirtsleeve, noticing that the bandage beneath was seeping fresh blood. "I could do with some new clothes and a better knife than the one I have. And a cutlass? Some new, comfortable, boots and a warm buckram coat?"

Puffing blue Sweet Virginia smoke into the night air from his pipe, Taylor chuckled as he said, "That'll lighten you of a few guineas. What about the rest?"

Jesamiah shrugged. He had no idea.

"Beware of wagering it away," Taylor advised. "Dice, horse racing, all those areas where chance comes into it is for fools. Cards, mind you, can be a different matter if you have the skill to play."

"Oh, I'm no expert, but I know card games," Jesamiah said. "To win, you need a clear head – drink and cards do not mix."

He grinned. "Although, it may be wise to not let your opponent be aware of that."

Puffing furiously at his pipe to keep it alight, Taylor said, when he had drawn enough life back into the bowl, "So, what games do you play?"

"Well, there's All Fours, Bassett, Ruff, Cacho, Flor, Cribbage, Gleek, Écarté…"

"Whoa, lad! Whoa! You good enough to play all of them competently?"

The grin broadened. "Mama said I am."

Disappointed, Taylor scratched at his chin. All doting mamas assumed their sons were good at everything. Aside, he could not believe a woman – a Spanish one at that – would know much about cards.

Tactfully, he said, "I reckon we'll put you to the test one day, but for now my advice is, don't risk gambling your money away. Invest it in a Goldsmith Bank. The Bank of England or Coutts. Safe as houses, they are."

Resting his arms along the taffrail, Jesamiah said with amusement, "The houses in Port Royal were not so safe. They fell down."

"Ah, but," Taylor argued, "they were not designed to finance a succession of wars, repay debt, or place a royal arse on the British throne – and keep it there."

Looking at him quizzically, Jesamiah asked, "Are you saying these banks are there to finance wars?"

"That is exactly what I am saying. And that is why the government is only too pleased to issue the likes of me with a Letter of Marque in order to keep their coffers filled." He tapped out the ash from his pipe. "Bank your money, lad. Save it for when you are a man grown and need it."

Taylor pushed away from the rail, stretched and announced he was for his bed. "Tomorrow, we'll sober that drunken lot up by making them haul our hard-gotten gains into our own hold, set the Spaniard ablaze, then head for the nearest port to celebrate properly. After that, we'll return to Jamaica and do our duty to m'sponsor. The bankers there will screw a fat profit out of you, but will take good care of what is left over." He was halfway down the companionway ladder when he said, without looking round, "We'll sail for Dominique first. It's mostly woodsmen and logging there, but I know of just the right lady who will fix that arm of yours more comfortable than Peterson ever can, and she'll sort out that manhood problem of yours at the same time."

25

___

DOMINIQUE, FEBRUARY 1709

Jesamiah rolled over, and groaned as sunlight buffeted him in the face. He rolled back, realised the comfortable bed was all his own, although there was a dent in the pillow next to him and the feather-filled mattress was still warm. Celebrating, he pondered as he stared up at the silk canopy above the bed, was all very well, but it left you with a sore head. He lay there for a few more minutes, intending to go back to sleep, but the urge to urinate was overwhelming. He threw the covers aside, ambled across the room and used the privy-seat in the side chamber – quite a luxury for this island, but then this whole house was one of no expense spared. His companion, he discovered, had returned while he had been busy relieving himself.

She did not appear to notice that he was as bare as the day he had been born, but then, why should she? They had both been naked since mid-afternoon yesterday.

"I 'ave brought us *le petit-déjeuner*, m' 'andsome, a *petit* something to give us energy for later, *non*?" She smiled at him, and he hurried forward to take the heavily-laden tray and set it on the table near the window.

Courteously, he helped her into one of the two chairs, then looked around for his shirt.

"Is something amiss?" she asked, lifting silver covers off the assortment of dishes.

"My clothes…?"

"Oh *la*, they are being, 'ow you say? Lindered? They will be returned soon." She was spreading butter on fresh, delicious-smelling new bread, and smiled. "It is more *délicieux* to eat without garments, is it not?" So saying, she set the knife and bread down and slid her silk robe from her shoulders, revealing her own nakedness.

Breakfast, Jesamiah decided, could wait.

DOLOREANA WAS HER NAME, BUT 'DOLLY' seemed more intimate, and intimacies had been abundant since *Mermaid* had dropped anchor in Dominique's harbour. Red-faced embarrassment had flooded Jesamiah's countenance when Malachias Taylor had ushered him through the doors into what seemed to be a palace. Gold-framed mirrors clad the walls, bronze statues of entwined, naked men and women, plush furnishings, crystal chandeliers. Silks, velvets, brocades, even Persian carpets on the floor. The women were as beautiful, fluttering around like an array of silk-clad, bejewelled butterflies.

"Madame Doloreana! Dolly, my dear!" Taylor, removing his hat, swept the one with hair as gold as the sun, and a bust amply protruding from her crimson silk gown, a deep bow.

"Captain Taylor," she purred in her enticing French accent as he kissed her hand, "you always promise to return, and you keep your promises, but oh *la*! The wait for you to do so, *monsieur*! The wait!"

"Well, my dear lady, I go where the wind takes me but this fine afternoon it has brought me, and my young friend here, to your forever-open entrance."

Jesamiah had reddened again as she glided over to him, her gown rustling, her wobbling bosoms surely about to escape the confines of her tight-laced corset. She looked him up and down as if he were an object for sale.

"You remind me of someone," she said, then noticing Taylor's swift shake of the head and finger to his lips, altered course. Taylor was perhaps right; it would not be wise to mention the name of the man she suspected, by the noticeable similarity of looks, to be this innocent boy's father. Instead she said, "Adonis. *Oui*, you remind me of the Greek god of love."

"I think you'll find, ma'am, that Adonis was Aphrodite's lover, he was not a god," Jesamiah said, feeling a deeper heat blush his cheeks.

She laughed and guided him towards the ornate staircase, his hot and sweating hand clutched in her cool grasp. "Then, Adonis, I will play the part of Aphrodite."

The bedroom at the top of the stairs had made him gawp in wonder. Opulent luxury was an understatement. The bed dominating the room was the largest he had ever seen.

She called for someone to fetch wine and food, and it occurred to him, after consuming quite a bit of both, that all this was going to cost a fortune. But, as she slid her silk garments from her exquisite body, such mundane thoughts had been instantly forgotten.

His first experience had been clumsy, quick and disappointing. She had smiled, stroked his hair and trickled her fingers down his chest and over his belly. "Now that the first *difficile* is over, I will show you 'ow to do it with more skill and satisfaction. *Non*?"

The 'showing' had been *très bon*.

26

Browsing the stalls and bothies arrayed along the harbourside, Jesamiah had already made several purchases: a new three-corner leather hat, three second-hand shirts and pairs of breeches which better fitted his maturing height and build, and a buckram longcoat that was also not new, but all it required were three missing buttons replacing. He bought a short dagger and sheath that fitted comfortably into the hollow of his back, and from the same trader, a fine-honed cutlass with a sturdy brass knuckle guard, its scabbard boasting an intricate pattern of birds in flight. To tame the hair on his face into what he considered to be the prospect of a rakish jawline beard and elegant moustache, he selected a fancy ebony box containing a shaving kit: a razor that was 'as sharp as a razor' – he had laughed heartily at the journeyman's joke – two bars of Castile soap, a leather strop, a small mirror and a pot of alum. Fitting neatly beneath the lid nestled a square linen towel.

Laden with his bargains, he stopped at one last stall, his attention caught by a set of brass buttons. Ah! Just what he needed for his coat! On peering closer, he was delighted to find that there were a dozen of them, all with an acorn design.

Perfect.

"I'll take them," he said to the woman behind the stall, who stank of body odour, fish and gin. "How much?"

She named a price, Jesamiah shrugged and felt in his pocket

for the required coins, handed them over and slipped the buttons into the same pocket. As he turned away, elegant fingers caught at his arm.

"They were overpriced, Adonis. You should 'ave bartered."

To his embarrassment, he felt himself stirring in his breeches at her nearness. He said hastily, "They are exactly what I want. I saw no point in attempting to beat her down."

Dolly laughed. "Traders will soon learn to love you, Jesamiah Acorne. As will the ladies." She flapped her hand in the direction of *Mermaid*, tugging restlessly at her anchor cable. "Malachias tells me you sail with the tide. You will come back to see me, *non?*"

Jesamiah grinned. *"Certainement, mademoiselle, certainement!"*

"Bon," she answered, "I 'ave grown most fond of you."

As I grew fond of your papa, she thought. She reached up and unthreaded the blue ribbon entwined in a lock of Jesamiah's hair. "I shall keep this," she said, putting the trophy to her lips to kiss it, then into the cleavage between her breasts. "To remind me of my Adonis."

She leant forward, kissed his cheek and whispered, "Malachias, 'e is a good man, but do not believe everything 'e says. Pirates are not truthful men."

Spinning around, she disappeared into the crowd. Jesamiah frowned, and muttered to her retreating back, "Privateers. We're privateers, not pirates."

He shrugged, then returned to the button-seller's stall. "How much for this blue ribbon?" he asked, picking up a reel of quarter-inch-wide royal-blue silk ribbon. *Jesamiah Blue,* Dolly had called the colour while romping together in her bed.

"Depends on 'ow much ye want of it," the crone responded.

"The entire reel." Jesamiah reckoned there were probably about two or three yards wound there. Again he felt in his pocket, brought out a few copper coins. "This'll do, I think."

The woman sniffed disdainfully; she had hoped for more, but then, she had already made a nice profit from those buttons.

27

PORT ROYAL, MARCH 1709

Malachias Taylor was in a foul mood. His banging about in the Great Cabin reverberated through the entire ship. He had been ashore for more than two hours, arguing with the customs and excise officer, and Jamaica's Governor, Major General Thomas Handasyd. When Taylor had eventually returned to *Mermaid*, he had slammed the cabin door and had been ranting there for a full hour since.

After a particularly loud crash, the men, finishing the tasks of leaving *Mermaid* shipshape before heading ashore with what they hoped was more money than could be stuffed into a threadbare pocket, looked concerned at each other.

"He's in a right tit," someone remarked, stowing a last bit of cordage. "D'ye reckon we're not goin' t'get paid?"

"Someone ought t'go down an' ask," another commented. "I ain't 'anging around 'ere working m'balls off if'n I ain't gettin' bloody paid."

"You will all get paid," Knucklebone Jake assured them, although even he wore a worried frown. He glowered at Jesamiah.

"Acorne. Go find what's got his prick in a twist."

"Me?" Jesamiah's protest came out with a hint of a youth's alarmed squeak.

"Aye, you, you bugger," Jake growled. "It's what you bleedin' get paid for."

"I don't bleedin' get paid for anything!" Jesamiah countered.

"That's because you never do as you're bloody told!" Jake retaliated, poking Jesamiah in the chest with one bony, tar-stained finger.

Tom Markham intervened. "Gentlemen! Gentlemen! Let us have calm here. Jes, lad, Taylor likes you. He'll not shoot you without reason."

That was not particularly reassuring.

"What if he has reason?" Jesamiah grumbled as he was pushed in the direction of the cabin door. He felt for the dagger nestling in the hollow of his spine, just in case. Palms sticky, a beading of sweat glistening below the flop of his forelock, he swallowed hard, then knocked once on the door, ready to spring back if a shot should tear through the wood.

Nothing happened, except the noise within stopped.

Jesamiah counted to ten. Knocked again. "Captain Taylor? Malachias?"

No answer.

"Sir? Are you alright, Cap'n?"

The door was suddenly flung open. Jesamiah retreated a hasty four paces.

"What ya want? Who is it?"

"Me, sir. Acorne."

There came a grunt, footsteps walking away from the door. "Come in, then; don't stand there like a naked, blushing virgin without a pimp."

Removing his hat, Jesamiah stepped through into the shadowed realm of the captain's cabin.

"And shut the bloody door."

Jesamiah shut it and stood just inside, twiddling his hat round and round between his fingers.

The place was a shambles; everything that could be upturned was upturned: books, charts, furniture. A pane of one stern window was broken. Glasses were smashed, navigation instruments were strewn among the debris. Several pieces of paper were shredded into strips; other documents were screwed into balls that were slowly unravelling themselves.

Dismayed, Jesamiah swallowed a despairing cry; it had

taken him hours to sort out those charts and paperwork. "Um… Is something amiss, Captain?"

"Amiss?" Taylor roared, swinging round to face him. "What makes you think that? Why would anything be amiss, eh?"

"Well, it's just that…" Jesamiah waved at the mess, lost courage and stuffed his hand into his pocket instead.

"It's just what?" Taylor growled, swaying slightly as he tottered across the room, broken glass crunching beneath his boots. He kicked an upturned stool aside.

Thinking it prudent not to answer, Jesamiah remained silent.

"I'll tell you what," Taylor taunted, shoving his face close to Jesamiah's, his breath reeking of rum. He was as drunk as a monk in a brewery. "I'll tell you, eh? I'll tell you what is amiss, shall I?" He flapped his hand at the shore beyond the stern windows. "Those two maggot-riddled, ball-less weevils that call themselves Her sodding Majesty Queen Anne's officers of the bleedin' law have cheated me, us, out of what is mine. Ours. That's what's bloody amiss!"

Jesamiah frowned, blurted out, "What? All of it?"

Taylor wiped his hand over his drawn face, righted a chair and sat, his shoulders slumped in weariness. "Nay, lad," he confessed, his voice quieter, defeated, "but my sponsor, Jamaica's governor, has elected to take an extra tenth on top of our previous agreed percentage."

Righting another chair and kicking debris aside with his foot, Jesamiah also sat, using the few moments to make a mental calculation. "Well, it's a lot but ain't so bad," he finally said. "It's a lower share-out for us all, but we had plenty in the first place."

"That," Taylor growled, "is not the point."

"I know it ain't," Jesamiah answered, bending down to pick up a piece of crumpled parchment, "but if we have no choice, why make such an Anne's Fan of it?"

Taylor released his tight breath in a slow sigh. The lad was right, but he had been so damned angry with Governor Handasyd and his skivvy, that sea-slug excise officer tosspot. Pay the requested amount or face the consequences. It stuck in the craw, but paying had been the only prudent decision.

"Amend the ledger as best you can without letting the men know they've been short-changed, will you?" he growled. "We don't want unnecessary trouble, do we?"

Jesamiah was turning the parchment the right way up, smoothing the crumpled wrinkles. He read a few words. "What's this?"

Taylor shrugged, stretched his neck and peered sideways at the writing. "Letter of Marque, by the look of it." He grunted as he stood up, opened a cupboard door. His temper had not been so great as to destroy his precious supply of rum and brandy.

"I can see it is a Letter of Marque," Jesamiah responded, barely hiding the tone of sarcasm, "but look, here." He pointed. "It is signed *William Rex III, 1698.*"

Not bothering with a glass, Taylor gulped brandy straight from the bottle. "I s'pec', then," he drawled, lurching back to the chair, "it's an old one. Prob'ly why I tossed it away."

"You do have another? A valid one signed by Anne Regina, or Governor Handasyd?"

Taylor frowned, offended. "O'course I do!"

"Where? I've never seen one among your papers."

"What's with all the soddin' questions?" Taylor roared, then belched and patted his side. "It's 'ere, in m'pocket. I keep it there to be at hand should I rec..." he hiccupped, "rec-require it." He belched again, grunted. His chin fell forward and within the next breath, a loud snore rattled from his nose.

Tossing the useless licence to plunder the enemy onto the table, Jesamiah removed the bottle from Malachias' hand, took several gulps of the liquor within before setting it down beside the captain's chair, and left.

He had a feeling that many of the crew would not be as philosophical as he was about receiving less money, but they would have more than enough to last them a few merry weeks. Aside that, apart from himself and Taylor, no one knew, even roughly, what each man was due. Not even Jake, for he had left all the tedious accounting to Jesamiah.

Back on deck, the crew were leaning over the rail, waving and cheering, eagerly watching a heavily-laden boat as it shoved off from the shore towards them. Chests of coin were stacked within, the exchange rate of silver for goods received.

Knucklebone Jake spat on his palms and rubbed them together in anticipation. "I'll set up the trestle table, Acorne, while you reckon what we're due. Mind you ensure your tally is correct, mark you."

What he meant was to mind that his own share was right.

Almost two hours later Jesamiah went up on to the quarterdeck, leant on the taffrail and watched the men as they took the gig and various summoned bumboats ashore. Dusk was falling. Torches were beginning to flare along the main harbourside thoroughfare, and candle and lamplight to spill from taverns, stores and brothels. Business was always busy when a vessel dropped anchor in Port Royal harbour, but for the time being Jesamiah had no intention of joining any shore-leave entertainment. He stared out at the higgle-piggle of buildings, thankful that they appeared to be remaining as nothing more than hastily-built taverns and tumbledown shacks, not a town of the past. He had money in his pocket-pouch, more stashed in his seaman's chest, but little inclination to spend it in case a mermaid or various ghosts were waiting for him. He would rather face that prospect come daylight, not during the hours of night.

DEVON

Spring was always busy where livestock was concerned. Lambing, calving, foaling. Tiola was only in her ninth year, but she had a knack with the ewes, cows and mares; she was a small, skinny child, but her calm voice and gentle hands soothed a distressed animal that was struggling through labour, and her maternal grandfather recognised a natural, God-given gift when he met it.

"She has a fine understanding of what be needed around beasts," Carter Trevithick said to his daughter. "She'll be a catch fer any farmer here abouts when she be grown."

"She's like my mother," Elswyth said, smiling with pride as Tiola at last succeeded in persuading a newborn lamb to suckle at her dam's teat.

"Aye, she be that," the elderly man agreed. "Your mam would be proud of her only granddaughter."

Elswyth glanced from her daughter towards the rugged stone church snuggled in a fold of the moor on the far side of the farm's boundary. Her mother, Tiola's grandmother, lay at rest in the churchyard there, although if her husband had managed his way, the woman's body would have been thrown over the cliff for the fishes to eat. They had not seen eye-to-eye, the two of them. The spitefulness of Reverend Garrick when he had gleefully told of the death of her mother – while she had been enduring the pangs of labour and bringing Tiola, their only daughter, into the world – had hurt then as much as it still hurt now.

Tomorrow was the last day of March and Easter Sunday. The day after, she, her daughter and two youngest sons, would be taking the dawn Flyer from Porlock to Truro, going back to Cornwall, back to her husband and back to the home that felt like a gaol more than home. Back to a husband who treated her as nothing more than a skivvy, and who made no secret, from her, that he preferred young, firm, women over the ageing ragbag that she had become.

What did he expect after the birthing of ten children? After the death of four of them, and several miscarriages in between? Her husband, for all his piety as a preacher, was a monster. Which is why she so enjoyed this annual visit to her widowed father's farm up here on the wild sweep of Exmoor, where the open moor rolled behind, and the open sea rolled ahead.

Elswyth's father patted her hand. He suspected the disharmony between his daughter and her husband, but honoured her stoic determination to make no public mention of it.

He nodded towards his granddaughter. "Your lass has the same skills as had your dear Mam. Mebbe even more so?"

Elswyth smiled at her father, but kept her thoughts to herself. Aye, and how long would it be for folk to start whispering about Tiola? Whispering that her gift was no gift, but the witchcraft of the devil?

29

LATE APRIL 1709

Boredom.

Perhaps, if Port Royal were the busy town it had once been, there would be plenty to do; time would not drag and lethargy would not have received a by-your-leave. But by the end of several weeks, the tedium had set in. When the weeks turned into a month and then another, the growing itch to return to sea had become as fevered and uncomfortable as a spreading, unwelcome, pox rash. Liquor had been sampled to excess, the whores in the brothels were losing their appeal, and more than a few of the crew were languishing in gaol. Two had been hanged: one for theft, one for murder.

Of Taylor, there was no sign or word. *Mermaid*'s oarsmen had taken him in the gig across to Kingston as mid-April had strolled in; the men had returned, he had not. The gnawing feeling that perhaps someone ought to investigate his whereabouts was rippling through Taylor's regular crew. The concern to investigate was genuine, though the impetus to do so had not reached beyond the thinking-about-it stage.

Sitting on a pile of fleeces awaiting sale by auction, Jesamiah was idly aiming pebbles at a hole in the quay's wooden boarding, his hat pulled low over his eyes to shield the glare of the evening sun. The thought that maybe someone should enquire after Taylor again entered his mind. What if he was in trouble? Injured? Dying? Surely someone would have sent word? If Taylor was in gaol, could a gaoler be bribed? Taylor had plenty of money, as did Jesamiah, although in those first few days it had taken over two hours at the bank to fill in endless forms, sign this, sign that, to see their share of the plunder secured in underground vaults. It had been the right thing to do, but Jesamiah was well aware that it would be even more difficult to get his money *out* again.

Aiming the last pebble, he smiled, satisfied, as it disappeared through the hole and plopped into the sea beneath. He got to his feet. Hands thrust into his coat pockets, he strolled away from the quay, heading for the sand-spit that served as a beach. The shoreline here shelved gently, making the depth of the tide alternate between shallow and deep; an ideal place to careen or repair. No one particularly cared that beneath the waves lay the ruins of the old town. He pulled his shoes and stockings off, walked on, and then sat cross-legged on the sand, still warm between his toes from the day's heat. The sun was disappearing below the horizon; he gazed at the sky as it briefly turned into a blaze of colour. He was missing the open expanse of the sea, the feel as it rolled beneath a ship, the sound as it churned past the hull. The euphoria he felt as the wind cracked in the sails or rattled through the rigging. The smells – the everything – of being at sea. He was enjoying sharing a bed with various Port Royal whores, on three occasions, two at once, but even the delight of sex was not the same as being out there on the ocean. Maybe when he met his own girl things would be different? If he were ever to meet her. And when he did, would he have to give up the sea?

He stretched out, put his hat down on the sand and linked his hands behind his head. The moon was rising, peeping out from behind dark streaks of cloud as if shy of showing her face. He closed his eyes. What did he want to do? What *didn't* he want to do? The second was easier to admit and answer. He did not want to spend his life plying up and down the coast of North America, trundling one cargo after another. Capturing that Spaniard had been invigorating and exciting, if fighting to save your own skin could be called exciting. He shifted his hips a little, and made himself more comfortable. Conceded a few more truths.

That Chase had been exhilarating. He had faced Death, that cloaked and hooded figure wielding a scythe and holding aloft a sand-timer; faced him, challenged him and won. The blood-pumped rush of excitement had been like a consuming madness, a could-not-care-less euphoria similar to being swamped by a surfeit of drink, or the climax of sex.

Drink, sex, fighting, sailing a ship; these were the things he wanted. Love? In time. Not yet. Money? Well, he had that. Maybe more would be worth getting? But that was not going to happen by idling here in Port Royal, musing and dozing on a beach beneath the moon, was it?

~ *Sailor?* ~

He opened his eyes, frowned, sat up, turned his head this way and that. Who had called? No one there. He lay back, closed his eyes.

~ *I can show you what you really want.* ~ A woman's voice in his head, seductive, like rich, velvet-smooth hot chocolate.

He felt a cool breath on the side of his face, fingers toying with his blue ribbon, then lips, tasting slightly salty, on his own, her tongue parting his mouth; burrowing deeper. A hand stroked his thigh, travelling higher to the buttons of his breeches. He dared not open his eyes to look.

~ *Get away from him, you crabmeat harlot! Get away!* ~ A man's voice; crisp, authoritative.

A scream. Feet scuffing in the sand and splashing into the water. Jesamiah's eyes snapped open. Had he fallen asleep? Been dreaming?

He got to his knees, stared around at the moon-shadows stretching across the beach. Not a soul was nearby. He stood, looked again. A group of men were on the quay some distance off. Were they beckoning to him? He stooped to pick up his hat, shoes and stockings. Someone was calling his name. He recognised Tom Markham's voice. Aye, those men were trying to catch his attention, best see what they wanted. Maybe Taylor had returned; decided it was time to set sail. Thank God!

~ *Seek me where the white rainbow kisses the sea.* ~

Three different voices swam in his head: a woman's seductive croon, his father's reprimand and the lilt of that young Cornish girl. Steadfast, Jesamiah shut all three from his mind, certain that if he ignored this insanity it would, eventually, go away.

30

———

"We've been looking for you, Jes," Markham shouted as he waited at the edge of the quay, one hand outstretched, urging Jesamiah to hurry. Knucklebone Jake and John Cleyver, *Mermaid*'s bosun, were with him.

"I've been on the beach," Jesamiah answered, although it was an obvious statement.

"Watching for mermaids?" Jake asked with a chuckle. "There's legend of one 'anging around 'ere. She lures unsuspecting lads into 'er arms, 'as 'er wicked way, then drowns 'em. Many a body 'as been found washed up on the sand along 'ere."

Expressionless, Jesamiah stared at him. Dare he admit he had – or thought he had – seen her?

"Don't fill the lad's 'ead with daft talk, Jake, we've more important matters to attend," Cleyver snapped.

Fists on hips, Jesamiah tilted his head back. "More important things such as what?"

"Such as, our Captain wants *Mermaid* taken across the bay to Kingston," Markham said.

"What – now? Why?"

Cleyver was already turning away. "Ain't your place to query or t'ask, boy. Get a move on, we've already wasted enough bloody time." He strode off, leaving the others to follow at a more sedate pace.

Tom Markham explained what little they knew as they walked. "He's sent a message asking for money. It seems our beloved Captain is losing at cards in some posh-rimmed Kingston gentlemen's club."

Jesamiah answered with a shrug. "Up to him how he wastes his money."

Markham scratched behind his ear. "That it is, but not when he's gambling against a scum-scut cheat."

"You can't prove that, Tom," Jake admonished, jumping in with a quick answer. "We all know you don't care a rotten, maggoty-piddled apple-core for Stannis."

"Stannis?" Jesamiah almost choked on the name. "What's the likes of him doing in a gentlemen's club?"

"Gentlemen and officers both. Been given the captaincy of the *Jamaica Rose*, the island's guard-ship. Didn't you know?" Surprised that Jesamiah did not, Knucklebone Jake flapped one of his hands landward. "His wife's been strutting around in fancy new finery boasting the fact, and that, consequently, they're moving across the bay to Kingston."

"It was news to me an' all," Markham said as they descended the weed-slimed wooden steps and climbed into the jollyboat bobbing on the swell at the bottom. Cleyver, already seated, grumbled at their dawdling.

"I didn't even know he had a wife. He don't seem bothered about spending much time with her, does he?" Jesamiah observed, tugging the painter free and shoving the boat off by pushing hard against the barnacle-encrusted support post, as Markham and Jake gave a hefty pull to the oars.

Cleyver guffawed loudly. "You clearly ain't seen or 'eard the wife! Looks like the wrong end of an 'orse, but she 'as money, see. That's why Stannis married 'er, oh, 'bout three, four year ago I think t'were?"

They settled into pulling steadily for *Mermaid*, the current strong, the wind buffeting waves and the side of the small boat. Jesamiah pondered an interesting thought: would he marry for money, or for a pretty face and love? He came to the conclusion that it probably depended on how much he needed the money.

31

KINGSTON, JAMAICA

Knucklebone Jake took a heavy pouch of silver to the club – and was refused entry. He returned to *Mermaid* expelling all the curses and oaths he could muster without taking breath. "Bloody wouldn't let me in. Said I were riff-raff, said I weren't dressed proper."

"They 'ad a point," Cleyver said. "I'm surprised they didn't mention you stink worse than a six-day-dead squid."

Jake mumbled something that sounded like, "They said that 'n all."

"Did you give the money to the doorman to give to Taylor, though?" Markham asked, folding his arms.

The whole situation was a waste of time. If they carried on like this for much longer, they would have no hope of catching a good tide. If that was Taylor's intention. The 'if' was a big one.

"No, I bloody didn't!" Jake snarled. "I'm quartermaster for a reason, an' one o' them reasons is that I know a thief when I look 'im in the eye. If I were t' 'ave left it with that muck-rudder, no one would've seen 'im or the money again."

"Why didn't you just demand that Taylor come to the door?" Cleyver growled, on the verge of losing all patience.

With an equally scathing expression, Jake glowered at him. "Now, why didn't I think of that? Of course I bloody asked – Taylor wouldn't come, 'e said 'e were busy an' young Jesamiah was to bring it instead."

Alarmed, Jesamiah immediately protested. "Me? Why me? I don't want no dealing with Stannis. Someone else can take it."

The quartermaster responded with a sound reason, prodding Jesamiah's shoulder as he spoke. "You've got some fine an' dandy new clothes stowed away, an' you can talk proper. Aside, it's Taylor's orders. No argument."

Jesamiah scowled, not liking the situation, but an hour later he stood, clean-shaven and well attired, beneath two tar-spitting lanterns illuminating the doorway to the prestigious St James Gentlemen's Club.

Looking surly and tapping a wooden club on his open palm, a burly doorman, more akin to an ape than a man, barred Jesamiah's way.

"Gentlem'n only, sailor. Be gone wiv ye." His voice matched his breath, as noxious as a bucket of rancid offal.

Enjoying the confidence that the sexual prowess of manhood had brought him, Jesamiah stood his ground, slid one hand into his pocket, and rested the other on the hilt of his cutlass. "I, sir, am the son of a Captain and a gentleman. That makes me, by birthright, also a gentleman. Now, step aside. I have business to attend within."

"What bizness be that, then?"

"My business, not yours." Irritably, in fluent French, Jesamiah ordered the man aside, partially sliding the cutlass from its scabbard as an extra reinforcement. The French worked, as, Jesamiah had recently discovered, it often did when used against lowlifes who could barely speak English, let alone any foreign tongue.

Within, Jesamiah handed his hat and cutlass to a servant; although reluctant to part with the latter, weapons were not permitted. He was not searched or asked to empty his pockets, however – who would dare be so insubordinate as to question a gentleman's honour?

Raucous laughter bellowed from a plush sitting room to the left. Several indelicately clad women were draped alluringly across chairs and couches, their attention applied to the men gathered around them. The gaming rooms would be quieter, less distracting.

"I seek Captain Taylor. Where is he to be located?" Jesamiah enquired. The servant pointed to the right. Jesamiah flipped him a coin. "Fetch me a brandy, a decent French."

The servant bowed, then scuttled away, and Jesamiah wandered casually into the card room, his narrowed gaze studying the two players at the nearest table. Watching the completion of the hand, which Taylor lost, Jesamiah grunted, walked forward and put the bag of coin down on the table in front of his captain.

Taylor looked up, startled, his eyes tired and red-rimmed, but grinned broadly when he saw Jesamiah. "Lad! Good to see you!" He stood, heartily pumped Jesamiah's hand.

"I'd advise you to settle your debts and leave now, Captain," Jesamiah answered, extracting his hand and not grinning. "Your ship, crew and tide await."

"Nay, nay, sit ye down in my place. Captain Stannis here has agreed to play one final game against you in my stead."

Finding himself pushed down into the chair, Jesamiah tried to protest. "I have no desire to play cards."

"Just one game. That's all. Your luck will be better than mine," Taylor persisted. "Here's my stake, Stannis." He shifted the bag of coin into the centre of the table.

Stannis took it, weighed it in his hand, assessing the contents. Nodded approval. "I'm 'appy to take money off your molly-boy as much as anyone else, Taylor. Does ye think 'e knows 'ow to play?"

"*He* knows how to play Dark Queen High, which as *he* observed, is your current game," Jesamiah drawled, irritated at being patronised. "Especially when it's not *his* own money *he's* using and *his* opponent stinks as much as an onion fart."

"He's deliberately riling you, Jes. Do not give him the satisfaction. Just play," Taylor interrupted. "The terms are that, if you win, Captain Stannis will relinquish all my losses."

"And what losses would they be?" Jesamiah asked, not caring to hide his annoyance as he picked up the cards Stannis had dealt.

Stannis chuckled, not a particularly pleasant sound. He brought a financial promissory note from his pocket, the sum named on it quite staggering, and a second piece of paper signed by Taylor. Jesamiah read it once, read it again, not believing the evidence before his eyes. He stared up at Taylor, who had the decency to flush and look guiltily away.

Incredulous anger got the better of Jesamiah's frayed temper. "You have gambled *Mermaid*? Lost her to this lowlife? I don't believe it. How could you be so inanely *stupid*!"

Taylor shrugged, embarrassed.

Stannis's chuckle deepened to a derisive guffaw. "Didn't expect to lose, did 'e? Nor did 'e stop to think that I'm amassing a sizeable fleet for the merchant business I'm now runnin', in addition t'bein' captain of the *Jamaica Rose*. With the acquisition of *Mermaid*, I can expand m'sugar an' baccy trade quite economically." He scooped up the two papers, folded them and slid them into his coat pocket, then picked up his own dealt hand of cards.

"Shall we play?"

Jesamiah won the first hand, lost the second, won the third, lost the fourth. Coincidence, or mere bad luck that, for each hand, despite there being the dummy kitty, he had been dealt the taboo card, the Dark Queen of Spades, for each losing hand? Come the fifth, which he also lost, he was certain Stannis was palming the card in his direction, but had no idea how to prove it. Again, he was dealt the queen and several disastrous high cards from other suits. Again he lost. One final hand – no queen but high cards, and Jesamiah lost. Stannis had the game. Taylor turned away, the colour of his face somewhere between ash-grey and sickly green.

Stannis gathered the discarded cards and his winnings. "I thought Taylor said you knew y'cards?" he sneered.

"I know them well enough," Jesamiah answered, biting back the additional words of *I also know you were cheating*.

"You were cheating." Taylor's fury was not as easily buried. "God damn you, you son of a bitch, Stannis, you were cheating!"

With calm ease, Stannis rose from the table. "I'll ignore the insult, Taylor, given you can't back your words with proof, an' that you're worse fer drink, but I advise you t'leave before I take offence. Tell your crew I'll be aboard an 'our afore the tide turns t'morrer."

Taking Taylor's arm, Jesamiah attempted to steer him away from potential conflict. "*Mermaid*'s crew will not sail with you, Stannis," he said, concealing his rage – a gift he had learnt so well when faced with Phillipe's cruelties.

Stannis stepped in front of them. "That'll be *Captain* Stannis, boy, an' there you're wrong. *Mermaid* an' 'er crew are mine t'do with as I will. M' first task'll be to instil respect. Something 'er previous owner were incapable of."

Taylor went for him. Snarling like a bear, he swung his fist and caught Stannis a glancing blow on the chin that sent him tumbling to the floor. Other men turned to see what the fuss was about, those who had been watching the game hurried forward as if about to protect the winner. Two startled servants rushed in, but Jesamiah, shoving Taylor aside, bent to assist Stannis to his feet.

"I have no liking for you, *Captain* Stannis, but I suppose I will have to accept you if you choose to come aboard." Almost reverently, he brushed a fleck of dust from Stannis's shoulder, then smoothed the man's ruffled waistcoat.

He offered a curt bow, then, without further word, turned on his heel and trundled Taylor from the club as if he were an inconsequential barrel of fish.

32

Within ten minutes they were seated in the jollyboat, Jesamiah rowing across the short expanse of sea towards *Mermaid*, Taylor sitting silent and morose in the bow. Fortunate, perhaps, Jesamiah needed all his breath for the oars, but his face and mouth were grim. Reaching *Mermaid*, he shipped the oars, grasped the ladder cleats and curtly gestured for Taylor to ascend. Securing the painter, Jesamiah followed in his wake.

On deck, Taylor went immediately to the rail and spewed over the side.

"What happened?" Markham voiced what everyone was wondering.

"What happened?" Jesamiah echoed, the held-in rage bursting from him. "This prize dolt of a drunken tosspot has lost this ship, that's what happened!"

"You!" Taylor turned around in red-heat fury, his finger, quivering in rage, pointing at Jesamiah. "You said you knew how to play cards! You fokken failed me. Us!"

Grasping the threatening hand none too gently, Jesamiah bellowed back. "I know how to play bloody cards. I know how to spot a cheat, but I do not know how to prove it, and it was not I who was idiot enough to gamble my ship away to a muck-rake like Captain sodding Stannis!"

A moment of stunned silence, then the entire crew began shouting and demanding an explanation, their rising fear of what was about to happen fuelling their anger. Taylor was shoved aside, someone kicked him. Harsh, unkind words were said. Someone else, Jesamiah had no idea who, even called for a noose to hang the bastard traitor. That sobered several of them, and they stepped aside, forming a circle around Taylor who stood, head low, tears of shame brimming in his eyes.

"I am not crewing under Stannis," Markham announced.

"You might not 'ave much choice," Jake said, gloomily.

"I've one very good choice," Markham countered. "I'm getting my things and going ashore. Jesamiah? You coming?"

Jesamiah shook his head, and said slowly, thinking things through as he spoke, "There are three choices, actually. Stannis is captain of the *Jamaica Rose*, and owns, from what I gather, other vessels?"

"Only one. The *Martha May*," someone answered.

"Or the *Martha May Not*," someone else laughed. Jesamiah looked puzzled.

"The wife's name is Martha May – 'er brig, left to 'er by 'er father. It's a standin' jest she don't permit Stannis anywhere near 'er bed, so it's *May Not*."

Jesamiah laughed, then returned to the serious business. "Our choices. One, abandon *Mermaid* and go ashore, try our luck with a different ship. Two, stay and serve under Stannis, or..." he paused, looked, one by one, at every man present, including Taylor. "Three, weigh anchor and get the fokking hell out of here."

They all stared at him in astonished silence. Was he mad?

"That would be open piracy," Taylor eventually said. "*Mermaid* is no longer mine, she belongs to Stannis. To take her would be to steal her. We'd all hang."

"Technically, aye," Jesamiah countered, "but has Stannis any way to prove, beyond doubt, in a court of law, that *Mermaid is* his ship?"

Exasperated, annoyed with himself as much as with Jesamiah, Taylor raised his arms, let them fall again to his side. "You know damn well he has! I have signed her away. Stannis has my promissory note of cash for the bank, and a bill of ownership for *Mermaid* for his lawyers."

Fumbling in his coat pocket, Jesamiah produced two pieces of folded paper and stuffed them both into Taylor's hand.

"You mean these?"

Taylor looked, bewildered, at the papers, at the writing, at the signatures. Looked again. Looked at Jesamiah. Looked at the crew, looked again at the two crumpled pieces of paper.

"How did you get these? How on earth…"

"Another thing my mother taught me," Jesamiah answered, breaking into a grin, "how to pick pockets. And no, do not ask how the daughter of a Spanish marquis knew how to do so. I never asked her, and nor will any of you ask me. Might I change the subject? I reiterate – shall we get ourselves out of here? Stannis will be somewhat annoyed when he realises he no longer has any proof whatsoever of ownership, and cannot do a soddin' thing about it."

33

'Somewhat annoyed' was an understatement, and although *Mermaid*'s crew did not have the pleasure, first hand, of witnessing Stannis's incandescent rage, they had a rough idea when shouts started echoing across Kingston harbour and several musket shots were fired haphazardly in their direction. When a cannon belched fire and smoke from atop the ramparts of the fort, the shot fortunately falling far short by over two hundred yards, the crew abandoned the capstan, cut the anchor cable and fled under full sail.

Mermaid was a fast ship with a diligent and willing crew of eighty-five men, but even so, for three whole days every one of them kept their eyes peeled on the horizon behind, anxious that Stannis could be coming after them in the *Jamaica Rose*. Fortunately, the *Martha May* was somewhere at sea, although, as a merchant, she would have been ill advised to go against a privateer.

Taylor, sober after four-and-twenty hours of snoring flat on his back in his cot, had laughed outright at the concern about the guard-ship.

"The *Jamaica Rose*? She's a fine enough vessel, but the sea-slops aboard her could not navigate their way across a puddle, let alone elsewhere, and she leaks like a cook's colander. Why do you think Governor Handasyd relies on the likes of us to keep his coffers filled with gold, not that lot of miscreants?"

"But Stannis is her captain now, he'll be raging about piracy…"

"Aye, but even he cannot patch gaping holes or sober up a drunken crew in a mere few hours."

"Aside," Jesamiah added, "on what grounds? Stannis cannot prove, beyond word of inebriated mouth, that *Mermaid* could be his. We are about our legal business sailing under a Letter of Marque. We are not pirates. Isn't that so, Captain?"

"That is indeed so. Indeed so," Taylor said, smiling at Jesamiah – pleased that the crew were reassured, pleased at this young lad's astuteness, although the 'lad' was rapidly maturing into manhood, in build, brain and ability – and showed signs of becoming a formidable opponent if riled.

Taylor cleared his throat with a loud *hrrmph*, rubbed at his whisker-stubbled chin and gazed for a few minutes at the set of the sails and the steady thrust of the wind behind them.

"First," he said speaking slowly, thoughtfully, "we need to get ourselves a replacement anchor, so we find ourselves a Spaniard or a Frenchie merchant. Something quick and easy to take."

He shrugged and waved one hand in a general seaward direction. "Shouldn't be no problem, but what legal business shall we be about after that, eh?" He tossed a sideways glance at Jesamiah as he said the word 'legal', but saw no flicker of reaction.

No one answered his question, so he continued. "I suggest we stay clear of Jamaica, even the Caribbean, for a while? If that be the case, we have several alternative options, the best two being we see what easy pickings there are along the Brazilian coast, or we can head east to the Africas. Either way, we are likely to come across something worth our while to invite ourselves aboard. And we will be well beyond Stannis's reach. What say you all?"

34

ATLANTIC OCEAN, JUNE 1709

They chose Africa, but to take their time and aim, first, for the islands halfway across the Atlantic, the Azores, where trade and treasure ships of all nations – British, Dutch, French, Portuguese and Spanish, depending on who was at war with whom – headed to replenish food, water and cargo. Privateers and pirates alike lurked in those waters, eager for an easy Prize or two.

With astute interest, Jesamiah passed his days by listening to all Taylor could teach him about sailing, navigation, wind, weather and the ocean currents. Listened, as well, to Taylor's knowledge of their intended destination.

"The Azores," Taylor explained one evening in the comfort of his cabin, brandy to hand, "is a Portuguese-owned volcanic archipelago. Most Atlantic shipping, sailing east or west, head for the island of São Miguel – St Michael – to replenish stores, make repairs and sample the local women and wine. In between us, though, is a little over one thousand miles of unpredictable ocean. An easy journey if wind, weather and tide are clement, not so easy if storms blow up or a wind does not blow at all. I've been becalmed for weeks with food, water and tempers fast running out."

Before setting off across the Atlantic, *Mermaid* had dropped anchor for three weeks at Barbados on the edge of the Windward Isles, checking for necessary repairs and provisioning with all that would be needed for the voyage. Despite being uneasy in enclosed spaces – a legacy from his half-brother, along with a dislike of anyone coming up quietly behind him – Jesamiah enjoyed the labour of hauling barrels, kegs, casks and crates into the hold. It was good to work below deck as one among the crew, to inhale the heady smells of pitch and coils of new rope and sailcloth, the stronger aromas of spices and pickled and salted food. Good, too, to spend nights ashore sharing laughter and drink with the men, with the intimate personal attention of the ladies.

With Barbados well behind them, the light winds became lighter, the calm seas calmer, *Mermaid* had been sailing sweetly, life aboard was pleasant and enjoyable, but with each hour, as the day grew nearer noon, their progress slowed. From her scudding through the great crests of white-capped rollers, *Mermaid* now ambled along, apparently unenthusiastic about reaching the Azores, let alone Africa. Even with every sail set, forming a pyramid of canvas from the largest to the smallest, even with the occasional drenching with buckets of seawater to stir a breeze among the spread of sail, *Mermaid* made snail's-pace progress. Yet the windless days were no great alarm. They had water, even if it was green and brackish, and food aplenty: eggs from the hens – or meat if one shirked her daily duty too often – milk, cheese and butter from the three nanny goats, Betty, Dolores and Fanny-Anne. Fish in the sea to catch.

Nor were they idle days for Jesamiah. He had Malachias Taylor's maps and charts sorted, studied, then stored, the piles of paperwork and documentation set orderly, with the Great Cabin itself following a semblance of tidiness, although pristine condition was a forlorn hope where Taylor's housekeeping carelessness was concerned. In between the charts and the paperwork, Taylor continued to teach Jesamiah how to fight. Not the fancy footwork of the rapier schoolroom, but how to fight to win, to save your skin and life. How to fight dirty if needed. Lessons with cutlass, sword and rapier; with long-bladed knife and short-bladed dagger, fist and feet. Swordplay, dagger play, wrestling. Day after day, practice and practice with

Taylor himself and the other men, until Jesamiah was as good as any one of them.

Their sessions were at dawn and dusk, when the heat was not so invasive, when the sails dripped with dew and the calm, blue sea was as smooth as a looking glass. There was nothing better, Jesamiah had discovered, when a vigorous sparring session was over, their semi-naked bodies slick, sticky and stinking with sweat, for he and Taylor to strip off their breeches and dive, naked, from the rail into that blue, blue sea, shattering the *Mermaid*'s almost-perfect reflection and the lazy stillness with their splashing and laughter. Among the men aboard, they were the only two who could swim. The others thought them a pistol short of powder, barking mad for enjoying the feel of the cold sea on their hot skin. Most seamen preferred to keep their bare feet firmly on deck. Who knew what was lurking beneath that deceptive calm?

When the wind did pick up enough to usher them forward with a slight curve to the sails and a faint cream of froth along the hull, they soon encountered floating mats of gold-coloured seaweed that enthralled Jesamiah. He had never seen anything like it.

"The Sargasso Sea stretches for several thousand nautical miles long, by several hundred wide," Taylor said as they leaned over the rail, staring down at nature's colourful spectacle.

"Will the rudder get snagged, or we get trapped in it?" Jesamiah asked, anxious. "Like a ship caught in ice?"

Taylor laughed, patted Jesamiah's shoulder reassuringly. "Nay, lad, the weed floats and parts before the bow as easily as does the sea. We will be fine – as long as we have a wind." He added the last with a frown, pleased to feel a slight caress of breeze on his cheek.

Here, in the Sargasso, the sea was even bluer, even clearer. Looking over the side one afternoon, *Mermaid* braced aback and hove to for the men to haul in a turtle caught for fresh meat, Jesamiah could see his own face staring back at him: black hair plaited into an unruly queue, the fuzz of a beard along his jaw, an embryonic moustache trailing each side of his mouth.

Frivolous, he waved at himself, and laughed as the reflection returned the gesture. He could see down and down into the depth well below *Mermaid*'s keel, twenty or so fathoms? A guess, of course, he had no idea. Fishes swam there, shoals flashed by full of swirling colour and movement. Then he drew back, his trance-like interest shattered by the shouts of his shipmates as they brought the hapless turtle aboard and called for Jesamiah to lend a hand to get it down into the stagnant water of the bilge. He was grateful for the distraction. He would not be looking, fascinated, down into the clear Sargasso Sea again. Would not be swimming in it, either.

His had not been the only face staring up at him from that depth of water, or the only hand waving. Pale skin, eyes as blue as the sky, golden hair – darkened by the water – floating in tendrils just as the Sargasso weed floated and swayed. A fish's tail that shimmered and glistened as if covered in a million, shining jewels.

The mermaid.

On the far side of the Sargasso, the wind gusting with more strength, they sighted yet another ship. Excitement flew around *Mermaid*'s decks, accompanied by laughter and chatter, with men leaning over the rail to point and look. Was she friend or foe? Was she a Spaniard coming into their clutches laden with treasure? Despite Taylor repeating, several times, that she might be Spanish but she was outbound so would not be carrying gold and silver, no one paid him heed. The disappointment was deep when she was identified as Dutch. Taylor would not touch English, Portuguese or Dutch shipping. Anything else was fair game. Except, nothing else appeared to be sailing neither east nor west across the Atlantic Ocean this June month of 1709.

An hour after dawn, two days out from the first of the Azore islands, another vessel was spotted – behind them, not ahead, and coming up fast. This time the activity was anxious, not excited. She could be a treasure ship, a trader, another privateer, or she could be Stannis come to find them and wreak revenge. Taylor, doubted it would be that bastard, but took prudent precaution by ordering the guns made ready and more sail set to take advantage of the sprightly wind. *Mermaid* was sleek and fast, but this vessel coming up behind was faster still. On edge, constantly looking over their shoulders or up to the crosstrees of the mainmast where Hench sat on watch, the men were restless. None of them cared a hoot for the risk of a fight, but it was the waiting that gnawed at the nerves and frayed them raw. What vessel was she? Why was she pursuing them so doggedly?

Then a laugh, a hearty cry plunged from the masthead, followed swiftly by Hench himself, descending hand-over-hand down the backstay to the deck, his face split from ear to ear by a wide grin.

"She's the *Barsheba*!" he announced. "It's Jennings!"

Whooping and cheering, they stood the guns down, took in sail and waited for Captain Henry Jennings to catch up; one of the best privateers in all the Northern Oceans, now that Charles Mereno had passed away.

There was celebration that night, with both vessels hove to alongside each other, and the Barshebas invited aboard *Mermaid* to partake of kegs of brandy and rum, for singing and merrymaking. Courtesy of fresh supplies donated by Jennings, the smell of roasting meat mingled with tobacco smoke and the stink of unwashed bodies. The carousing reached as high as the stars, and even the moon did not dare show her face from behind a curtain of cloud for fear of watching too closely the antics of drunken pleasure-taking.

In Taylor's Great Cabin, the papers and charts had been hurriedly put away, the table pulled out and set for a lavish, celebratory meal. The linen tablecloth, silver tableware and dinner service was displayed to fine grandeur, despite the plates and serving dishes bearing all too many cracks, chips and scratches. Pork, chicken, fish. Vegetables, sweetmeats, dried fruits. Wine, port, brandy. The conversation and laughter grew louder with each dish served and consumed, each glass poured.

As quartermaster's clerk, Jesamiah had been invited to join the dinner party, but was awed by the auspicious company and the fact that he was seated almost against the brooding figurehead dominating the far corner. He did not like the thing.

Jennings was next to Taylor, but with only a handful of diners, was close enough to engage in conversation with Jesamiah, when finally he had opportunity.

"So, you're Charles's boy? Jesamiah Mereno?"

Jesamiah's skin tinged a salmon pink. "I go by the name Acorne now, sir. Jesamiah Acorne."

"Fair enough," Jennings responded, lifting his half-empty glass in salute. "There's many of us, for various reasons, using a different name to the one we were christened with."

"Especially where avoiding a wife, the law, or service to the Navy are concerned, eh?" Taylor laughed.

"Indeed," Jennings answered, "and many another will be following suit when this war with Spain ends, I reckon." He raised his glass, proposing a toast. "To alternative identities – may they never be revealed!"

"May they never be revealed!" The cheer echoed through the ship, although none beyond the Great Cabin could hear, for the noise the crew were making was too rowdy.

A short while later Jennings resumed his conversation with Jesamiah, a friendly smile playing over his features. He was about mid-forty years of age, Jesamiah reckoned, no longer carrying the slender figure of a young man, but not yet running to fat. His eyes held laughter, but there was a sterner side to him behind the smile. A formidable man when the need arose, but perhaps a good friend also?

"I knew and respected your pa, son. It is a pity you no longer wish to carry his name, but I can see that Mereno could also be a burden to you. Sometimes it is best not to sail too close in another's wake."

Jesamiah made no answer; he was not prepared to whine about his childhood to this man, even if he was a friend of Taylor and his father.

Jennings carried on as if there were no secrets to be hidden away. "We did everything together, didn't we, Malachias? You, me, Charles and Morgan – before the drink and the infatuation with that girl blew up into a row."

Looking up sharply from the glass of rum he had been studying, Jesamiah blurted out, "Girl?"

Taking the wrong meaning, Jennings grinned. "Don't get all heated, lad. I was referring to Morgan's harlot, not your father's. Oh, Charles was one for the ladies, mark my word," he laughed, and winked at Taylor. "Weren't we all back then, when a night in bed meant more than getting some sound sleep!"

"Speak for yourself!" Taylor's guffaw boomed out. "I'm still able to be partial to the services of a woman."

"Aye, to keep your feet warm, not your other shrivelled piece!" Jennings tossed back.

Everyone laughed, but by the time glasses had been refilled and talk resumed, the subject had changed. Jesamiah was left wondering, his question unanswered. Did Captain Jennings mean this mermaid creature? Was she Morgan's harlot? Surely not – not when there had been whores a-plenty filling the brothels and streets of Port Royal.

'There are no such creatures as mermaids,' he told himself as he tossed back another glass of rum.

And yet... and yet...?

36

With most of both crews drunk, few were left on deck to keep an eye on wind, sail and sea. If this was the Navy there would likely be floggings all round, but privateers held to their own rules. Many a ship went down or caught fire because of inebriated revelry; even Morgan had lost his flagship on one of his expeditions to raid the Spanish-held South American coast. And not just the ship. The powder magazine had caught alight; dozens of good men had been killed because of a moment's rum-riddled negligence.

Jesamiah had downed a few drinks – rum, wine and port – but Jennings' presence had unsettled him and he had partaken of nothing more after the meal had finished. What had he meant by 'infatuation with that girl'? Perhaps, more worrying, as he sat huddled in a corner of the quarterdeck sheltered from the cold wind that had risen steadily through the night, was the fact that he too was becoming infatuated with her?

When he closed his eyes to sleep, the mermaid was there in his dream. That alluring smile, her slender fingers beckoning, her wet hair shining in the moonlight.

And then the other girl was there also, the Cornish lass. She always seemed agitated, was she trying to warn him? Against what? The mermaid? The sea? Jennings? Someone, something, else?

In his dreams Jesamiah could barely hear her, as if she were calling from a long distance away.

~ *Tiola* ~ was all he could hear her say.

~ *I am Tiola.* ~

37

A sound woke him. He opened his eyes, narrowed them as a wave of outrage swept through him and he scrabbled to his feet.

"Oi! You! Piss over the side, not on our deck. Or do it aboard your own bloody boat!"

The man, continuing to stream his urine onto *Mermaid*'s deck, glowered over his shoulder, his features contorted in contempt. "I'll piss where I want t'piss, boy." The insult stung, for the culprit was only about three years Jesamiah's senior.

"Not on this vessel you won't, *boy*," Jesamiah retorted, his fists bunching at his sides.

Finished, Charles Vane buttoned his ragged and stained breeches and turned towards Jesamiah. Folding his arms, his head on one side, his sneer was as nasty as a murderer's grin. "So, what are you goin' t'do about it?"

Jesamiah moved fast. Taking Vane completely by surprise, he cannoned into him, shoulder first, knocking him off balance and to one knee. Vane twisted around, a knife coming into his hand, a snarl leaving his lips, but Jesamiah had anticipated the move, kicked out and caught Vane's jaw, sending him sprawling into the puddle of urine. Not giving ground, Jesamiah knelt on him, pinning him down, riding out Vane's anger and his attempts to buck his opponent off. They were evenly matched; similar age, height and build, but there the likeness ended. Vane enjoyed brutality. He delighted in the power he held over others and in delivering pain and terror to those who could not fight back. Jesamiah knew his sort. He had lived with Phillipe for just under fifteen years. Added to that, Vane thought he needed no tuition from old men who were past their prime. Unlike Jesamiah, who wanted to learn all he could from whoever would teach him – tutoring which included the art of fighting to stay uninjured or alive.

"You are a guest here," Jesamiah hissed as, one-handed, he tugged his blue ribbon free from his hair and, releasing the grasp he had on Vane's collar, looped it around the man's neck. "Add to that, I am no 'boy', and you will…adhere…to… our…rules."

The ends of the ribbon held tight in each hand, Jesamiah crossed his arms at the elbow and steadily tightened the improvised garrotte with each enunciated word. Within a few heartbeats Vane's face was shading into a puce-red, his eyes were bulging, his tongue was poking from between lips that were starting to bear a blue tinge. Jesamiah pressed his knee further into Vane's spine, tightened his grip on the ribbon. A few more tugs would strangle the bastard, or one quick downward thrust with his knee could break the man's back.

"Alright, lad, you've made your point. Let him go." Henry Jennings said from a few paces behind.

Jesamiah ignored him.

"I do not have so many skilled topmen that I can afford to lose one to your sense of justice, Acorne. Let him go. Or are you as callous a killer as is he?"

Still Jesamiah held his blue ribbon around Vane's neck, the responding gurgles becoming more desperate.

~ Let him go! ~

Words in his head. His father's voice. Jesamiah released his held breath – although he had been unaware that he had been holding it – and simultaneously let go of one end of the ribbon, slid it from Vane's neck and shoved it into his waistcoat pocket. He stood up, breathing heavily, nostrils flaring, anger flaming in his eyes.

"Swill your mess away, Vane," Jennings ordered, "mind your sodding manners, and get yourself over to *Barsheba*."

Vane got to his knees, a thin, vivid red weal around his throat; he glowered at his captain, noticed the dagger dropped to the deck and roared with rage as he grabbed it, leapt to his feet and struck out at Jesamiah, who, neatly stepping aside, was once again quicker.

Grabbing Vane by the hair, Jesamiah punched him in the belly, winding him, swung him to the rail, kicked him, hard, in the back of the knee, hooked his arm between his splayed legs and heaved him upwards so that he dangled precariously over the rail.

"Don't, Jes lad," Jennings advised. "He can't swim, and I don't want to have to send you in to save him."

"Who said anything about saving?" Jesamiah retorted.

Jennings shrugged. "'Like I said, good topmen are difficult to come by. Let the bugger go."

For several long minutes Jesamiah held his victim where he was, then abruptly hauled him off the rail and dropped him to the deck.

Jennings peered down at him. "You're not worth your own piss, Vane. Do as I order or I'll maroon you."

Scowling, Vane scrabbled to his feet and scuttled away, several men who had gathered to watch jeering at him.

"You've made an enemy there, Acorne," Jennings observed as he stepped up into the chains in order to relieve himself over the side. "Be careful of him. He'll not forget this."

Eye-to-eye, Jesamiah gazed, unafraid, back at the older man. "So has he made an enemy. So will he need be careful. And neither will I forget. Sir."

38

PONTA DELGADA, SÃO MIGUEL ISLAND, OCTOBER 1709

Working in consort, *Mermaid* and *Barsheba* plundered five Spanish and three Frenchies as they made their leisurely way in and out of the islands, occasionally dropping anchor to replenish fresh water and hunt for fresh meat, once to take advantage of a sheltered bay to wait out a passing storm; another time to make minor but necessary repairs caused by an aggrieved French ship.

After the fierce altercation with the fifth Spaniard – they had put up a good fight before surrendering – Jesamiah was beginning to regard himself as a seasoned privateer. The fear of battle no longer turned his guts to water.

With the prospect of gold in their pockets and the stores yet again running low, Jennings and Taylor had declared it time to make use of their gained spoils and partake of a more leisurely life for two weeks at the Azores' harbour town of Ponta Delgada. The two weeks had lengthened to four, the four to eight, the eight to ten...September had quietly stolen in over one horizon and left across another.

São Miguel Island. Green, pleasant, wide flat valleys at the foot of the mountains, dominated by the volcanic peaks, caressed by a blue sea and carpeted by exotic flowers of brilliant hues. Exotic birds fluttered through trees laden with fruit, the citrus smell of ripe orange and lemon intoxicating to the senses.

The first few days ashore, Jesamiah had been reminded of Shakespeare and Prospero's island, a quotation from *The Tempest*, one of the plays he had enjoyed reading, and partially acting, with his mother: *Sounds and sweet airs that give delight and hurt not.* Until a strong wind gusted from the mountains and the pleasantness was tainted by the whiff of bad-egg sulphur from the hot-water springs bubbling up through the ground.

For the port of Ponta Delgada itself, the narrow, cobbled streets were enticing, especially the market, taverns and 'lady lanes', which drew the seafarers' attention more than any visual or culinary delight.

Sauntering down one of the side streets one night after a few glorious, and satisfying, hours in the company of one such delight, Jesamiah was deciding whether to return to *Mermaid* or seek the pleasure of another few drinks in one of the harbourside taverns. He reached the main street, and stood a moment deliberating over which tavern. The Jack Tar served good ale but watered-down rum, the Cock and Bull – officially Ball, but one of the religious groups had insisted on the less suggestive name – had too surly a landlord. The Jolly Boat harboured too many Royal Navy tars...it would have to be the Buxom Wench, although most of the men called it the Two Tits.

He thrust his hands into his coat pockets and lengthened his stride, gaze fixed on the more than amply proportioned woman painted on the sign swinging above an open doorway at the far end of the wharf. Light spilled from the other taverns. With half a dozen ships resting at anchor in the harbour, the streets were busy with life. He walked past the Admiral, more of an officer's club than a tavern, though the noise coming from within was as raucous as any frequented by seamen. He passed a side alley, glanced up it, vaguely noting shadows moving in the dim light from two smoking torches in doorway wall sconces. Whores would be plying their trade up against the dank walls, the grunts testament to men partaking of their pleasure.

It was only two strides further on that Jesamiah realised the shadows had not been the right shadows, the grunts not the right grunts. He partially drew his cutlass, retraced his steps, stood at the alley entrance taking in the flickering movement with the briefest of observations.

Six men, Navy by the look of them – sailors had a knack for knowing Queen Anne's men when they saw them. Six men vigorously – but beyond the grunts of expelled breath, the scuff of feet and thuds of fists on flesh – soundlessly beating up one other. Jesamiah hesitated. This was not his fight; no doubt the one receiving a thrashing deserved it. He turned to walk away, leaving the Navy scum to get on with it, then turned back at the blasphemous curse that ripped into the night air. He would recognise that voice anywhere, for the more usual reason of avoiding it as diligently as staying away from the plague.

Vane. Charles bloody Vane.

For two seconds Jesamiah considered joining in with the Navy thugs, but honour and conscience got the better of him. The Royal Navy made fun of the Merchant as a matter of course, and privateers even more so. There was no love lost between any of them. To settle on the side of the Navy? Jesamiah would rather be nice to his half-brother, and given that was as unlikely as hell freezing over…

Without further thought of what he was doing, he drew his cutlass and, with a roar of indignation, hurtled into the affray, slicing his blade from left to right through the woollen jacket, skin and muscle of one man's back, severing his spine, then on the downward, opposite thrust, into the side of the next man's neck. Semi-decapitated, the jugular ripped open, he died quickly, choking on his own blood. A third sailor turned, startled by the unexpected attack, and reeled backwards as Jesamiah's basket knuckle guard, made of solid, heavy brass, slammed into his jaw, shattering the bone. The fourth, distracted, found Vane, who had been curled up protecting himself from the worst of the blows, coming upward, fists bunched, pounding, one-two-three, into his belly. Winded, he fell to his knees and Vane brought up his foot to stamp hard on the man's neck, snapping it as easily as if it were a dried stick. The last two, the younger of the group, fled up the alley, their feet scrabbling on the cobbles. One made the mistake of looking back over his shoulder. Vane had found his dagger, dropped in the first few moments of the fight, and the boy – for that was all he was – screeched, turned and ran after his crewmate, but was too late. Vane threw the blade, the glinting steel whistling as it sped through the air, the thud sickening as it ploughed into the boy's back. The squelch even more so as Vane sauntered over and jerked the knife out, leaving the boy to bleed to death or drown in the blood filling into his punctured lung.

Without glancing at Jesamiah, or even acknowledging his presence, Vane rolled each body over, ensuring no one lived, and relieving any pockets of anything worthwhile in the process. The last man he checked was the one with the severed spine; his eyes were open, gurgled words were coming from his mouth. Vane jerked his dagger blade through the unfortunate's throat. The gurgling increased for a few seconds. Stopped.

Bending over, Vane wiped his dagger on the dead man's shirt, sheathed the blade and after pocketing a cheap watch, some coins and a gold earring which he yanked free, he began to walk away.

"A thank you would not go amiss," Jesamiah stated, putting on a show of cockiness as he bent to wipe his cutlass clean, hoping Vane would not notice that he was swallowing down an urge to regurgitate his supper. Killing men for the sake of it, and for someone else's fight, was something completely different to killing a man in order to keep yourself alive.

"I ain't wastin' no thank yous, nor is I 'angin' about 'ere," Vane retorted. "One got away. If 'e fetches 'is mates from the *Bonney Chance*, you'll be danglin' from a yardarm before the 'our's up."

Jesamiah saw his meaning and, thankful for the excuse to leave, followed in Vane's wake, heading for the anonymity of the *Mermaid*.

"An' you better 'ope, Acorne, that lad don't recognise you ag'in," Vane added as they hailed the *Mermaid*'s jollyboat to come fetch them.

"He's more likely to recall you," Jesamiah pointed out. "You were the one they set upon." He did not bother asking about whys and wherefores, guessing that Vane would never condescend to offer an explanation.

Vane grunted as he strode into the shallow water, ready to step into the ship's small boat as soon as it arrived.

"Maybe take the opportunity to clean yourself up while you're waiting?" Jesamiah suggested, indicating the blood oozing down Vane's face. "I'll hold your breeches' waistband if you're scared you might drown."

Another grunt, but Vane took the advice about the washing, although not the assistance.

WHEN THE BLOODIED bodies of the murdered men were found and identified, there came an outcry from the naval ship's captain. He sent his officers to enquire, with stern authority, if there were any bloodstained and bruised sailors aboard any of the vessels anchored in the harbour. A futile exercise, for sailors were notorious for getting into fisticuffs and there was no way to prove which particular altercation was which. All the same, the captain placed a formal protest with the island's governor, along with an addendum that, should the perpetrators be discovered, they would hang. As for the rest, replacement tars were found, and HMS *Bonney Chance* sailed away, her officers none the wiser, nor especially concerned beyond indignation at the slight towards the service. Neither Jesamiah nor Vane spoke of the incident to anyone, although there were more than a few sideways glances at the cuts and bruising Vane sported.

For Jesamiah, he had not stopped shaking through what was left of that first night as he lay in his hammock slung on the lower deck, the hatches above wide open for air and coolness. He had ignored the churning in his belly while about his chores, when it was necessary to keep bravado etched onto his face, but as he lay staring up at the stars, mouth dry, stomach again threatening to regurgitate into his throat, the trembling had returned. He argued with himself – had he walked away, Vane would be the one dead and weighing heavy on a questioning conscience. Had he been walking along a few minutes earlier it could have been himself those scumslugs had attacked. The arguments were sound, but the shaking did not ease until the sun was high over the main brace and the *Bonney Chance* had disappeared from sight.

Three days later, *Mermaid* and *Barsheba* set sail to resume their joint patrolling for unsuspecting Spaniards and Frenchies. Jesamiah did not forget his first real, bloody fight for the sake of a fight, but there were now other things to be thinking of. Hunting lucrative prey being the prime one.

39

CAPE VERDE, AFRICA, OCTOBER 1710

Mermaid and *Barsheba* prowled the seas around the Cape Verde islands together for twelve months, occasionally venturing closer to the African Guinea coast or heading northward towards the Canaries, taking their leisure in between voyages to careen or enjoy the delights on offer at various ports. The French and Spanish were a nuisance to the locals, preying on Portuguese settlements and attacking with impudence. Knowing these privateers were dealing out a taste of the enemy's own medicine made the two crews more than welcome wherever they dropped anchor – it seemed the hostile raiding by Francis Drake, who had sacked Ribeira Grande twice in the late 1500s, had either been forgotten or forgiven. But as the months passed and word of the English presence spread, suitable Chases became more difficult to find, until a Spanish trader, the *Santa Cecillia*, came along...

The Chase done, the Prize captured, smoke drifted lazily from the smouldering remains of what had been her neat and trim quarterdeck. Jesamiah, equally lazily, rested his arms on her main deck rail and watched, with fascination, as the sharks finished what was left of the bloodied corpses tossed overboard. Their own dead, those killed by cannon fire and pistol shot during the vicious fight, would be sewn into canvas shrouds weighted with a heavy ball and receive Christian prayers as they were committed to the deep. The Spanish did not deserve the same respect. They should not have put up a fight; those who surrendered, lived, those who didn't, didn't. It was as simple as that. The *Santa Cecillia* had led the privateers a merry dance for more than three days, trying every trick to lose the two dogged vessels. To no avail, but then, the Spaniard was not captained by Malachias Taylor or Henry Jennings.

According to her logbook, the *Santa Cecillia* had voyaged from Madagascar via the Cape of Good Hope, carrying a wealth of cargo: timber, tea and ivory, spoils that now belonged to the crews of *Mermaid* and *Barsheba*.

This was their last attack together. Jennings was to take *Barsheba* to the Arabian Gulf, where money could be made raiding the rich Muslim ships. *Mermaid* was to head home to the Caribbean.

"You are welcome to sail with me," Jennings said, coming to lean on the rail next to Jesamiah, his nose wrinkling at the sight of gorging sharks.

The offer was tempting, but there were buts, not least of which was the fact that Jesamiah did not fancy sailing with Vane. "I thank you for the offer, Captain, but would you make me quartermaster's or bosun's mate?"

Jennings laughed, pressed his hand onto Jesamiah's shoulder. "Next in line for either will be Vane. I do not trust him but he is capable, so no, alas, I cannot tempt you with that particular bribe."

"There you go, then. Taylor could offer me an opportunity when we reach Port Royal. Cleyver has decided to hang up his hammock, and I reckon Tom Markham will be favoured as our new bosun, then I might be considered as his mate, although being a topman and clerk to the quartermaster suits me well enough for now."

"Cleyver's going ashore, eh? He has a wife in Jamaica, several sprogs also, I believe. Don't blame him for returning home," Jennings said. "I've land there as well, you know. A plantation I inherited from my wife, though it don't yield much. Ground's too sickly."

This was news to Jesamiah. "I didn't know you had a wife?"

"She died giving birth to our first child. A daughter. She died too."

"Oh. I'm sorry."

Jennings shrugged. "It was a long time ago, a lot of tides have turned since then. My youngest brother and his wife manage the plantation. He is a better farmer than I and, frankly, they are welcome to it. Last I heard, he was growing oranges, lemons, pineapples and such. Apparently, there's a good market for fruit."

"Do you not miss your wife?" Jesamiah asked, thinking incongruously of his father. Had *he* missed *his* wife?

"Wives?" Jennings chuckled. "They celebrate their husbands spending long months at sea. It means no worries about another swelling belly, and for us, well, ain't that what whores are for?"

Somehow, Jesamiah could not picture Henry Jennings with a woman. Did men his age have sex? A thought passed briefly through his mind about begetting children. Since that first thrill of Dolly's bed, he had taken pleasure with many women. He had never considered the possibility of children, though. Ah, but they had all been street doxies, and hadn't someone told him that children were only blessed on married couples, and that doxies were infertile? Somehow these facts didn't sound right, but Jennings had changed the subject.

"I will expect to see you a captain before long, lad, though I advise you to stay out of trouble. Privateering is all well and good but this war about who is to sit his arse on the Spanish throne will not last much longer. When peace comes, there will be no need for us buccaneers. Find yourself a suitable merchant business and work hard at that. Don't be tempted into piracy."

Jesamiah said nothing.

"You've the finances to start your own trade, Jesamiah. Probably enough to purchase your own ship."

At that, Jesamiah laughed. "Oh aye, I have some gold stashed in a couple of banks dotted here and there, but that's all. Hardly enough to buy a ship!"

Jennings' turn to guffaw. "Nay, son, your father had stuff stored in warehouses all over the place. Quality stuff."

"My father," Jesamiah retorted with a snort of scorn, "left

everything to my bastard half-brother. I saw not a penny piece of anything."

"Ah," Jennings rubbed the side of his nose, "as far as I knew, the warehouse contents were to be yours. Does your brother know of them? If not, just go in and take what you need."

Another wry laugh, and Jesamiah's turn to pat Jennings on the back. "Without proof of ownership, wouldn't that constitute an act of piracy?"

"Aye, but—" He did not get any further. A loud noise, shouting, the sound of something heavy being knocked over echoed through the stricken Prize, coming from the direction of the hold.

"What are they doing?" Jesamiah grumbled, abandoning the conversation and pushing away from the rail. "If they've found more drink and are squabbling over it, Taylor isn't going to be amused. We've spent long enough aboard this vessel as it is."

With Jennings striding in his shadow, he went towards the open hatchway, a few of the crew also wandering over to peer down into the semi-gloom of the below-deck world.

A shot. Another. Within an instant the air of relaxed ease changed to on-guard wariness.

"What's goin' on down there?" the bosun, Cleyver, shouted, concerned, into the open hatch, as men ran to join him, weapons coming to hand.

A third shot, a wild scream, scuffling; then all went quiet.

Pistols cocked, a few men hurried down the ladder, Jennings and Jesamiah peering after them as Taylor pushed everyone aside to descend the ladder as well.

"Be careful," Jesamiah warned unnecessarily.

"What's happening here?" Taylor's voice was cross and impatient as he disappeared into the darkened hold. "All you had to do was transfer cargo, can I not rely on you drunken sots to…Oh God! Jesus bless us!"

Taylor reappeared, face ash-grey, agitated. Peering up into the sunlight, he saw Jesamiah leaning down, and ordered abruptly, "Find Surgeon Peterson!" Then disappeared again.

"I'll go! He's in his quarters on *Mermaid*," O'Bartlett said, hurrying off.

Two men staggered up the ladder, one bleeding from a slash across his cheek, the other nursing a shoulder wound. "Bastards were hiding behind the last of the cargo," one cursed, "waitin' for us."

The body of a dead man followed, hoisted by Taylor and others who had gone to help. Cleyver, *Mermaid*'s boatswain. A bullet clean through his forehead. A swift death, he would have known nothing about it. A fourth man was being carried up, his face white, his lips turning blue. Blood was seeping through his shirt. Jesamiah's own face drained pale as they laid the dying man on the deck.

"Tom? What happened?" Jesamiah knelt down, took his friend's hand in his own, choking back distressed tears as he spoke. "Tom? Hold on, mate, Surgeon Peterson's coming."

Tom Markham opened his eyes. Blood was bubbling at the side of his mouth, his breath coming in short, laboured gasps. "I'm done for, Jes. Say a prayer for me. Take care of yourself, you're a good lad."

He closed his eyes. Life passed from his mangled body with his last breath.

Jesamiah bowed his head and didn't care who witnessed him weeping.

40

ATLANTIC OCEAN, NOVEMBER 1710

"See anything?"

Jesamiah looked up as Taylor, out of breath, seated himself beside him on the limited space of the crosstrees.

"Shift up, lad."

Obligingly, Jesamiah moved a couple of inches.

"I've not been up here in...phew," Taylor puffed air out of his cheeks, "many a month." He patted the thickening expanse of his belly. "As you can see."

"So, what brings you here now?"

"Oh, just wondering if you'd seen sight of anything." Taylor tapped the book Jesamiah had been reading. "Or whether you would notice a galleon passing direct astern, you being so engrossed in whatever it is you are so engrossed in."

Jesamiah held the book up for Taylor to read the title embossed on the brown leather cover. "*Pilgrim's Progress*. Not quite my taste, but did you know Bunyan wrote it while imprisoned in Bedfordshire gaol?"

Taylor shook his head. He was not one for literature.

"Shows there's hope for us all," Jesamiah added. "We can achieve something, even in gaol."

"I don't need a written book or a boring preacher to tell me that," Taylor chuckled.

A pause, a long silence.

"I finished sorting that paperwork of yours, yet again, this morning while you snored in your bed," Jesamiah stated. "I wish you'd leave the bloody accounts to me. You and Jake, when he bothers, make such a mess of them. We're getting low on water and there's no more salt beef."

"Well, you were busy and—"

"I'm only busy because I keep myself busy," Jesamiah snapped.

"Aye, I know, and I appreciate it, but, well, I've not heard you laugh for weeks now."

Jesamiah indicated the sullen sails. "Wind is uncooperative, water running out, stores getting low. Not much to laugh about, is there?"

Taylor sighed. How was he going to jostle young Acorne out of this moroseness?

"Look, I know Tom was a friend, but life's short and death is inevitable. Night, day, birth, death. We have to accept it all for what it is."

Jesamiah closed the book, unsure why he was reading it. He stared outward across the ocean. They had passed south of the Sargasso Sea, the wind intermittent, but the Windward Islands were ahead, four, five days?

"It all seems so pointless," he admitted. "I'm amassing a fortune, but to what benefit?"

"Your benefit, lad."

"Oh, you mean one day I will meet a girl, fall in love, lose her in childbirth and end up dead like Tom or Cleyver?"

"No, I mean one day you might meet a girl, fall in love, settle down and become Governor of Jamaica like Henry Morgan did."

That made Jesamiah laugh, although it was a cynical guffaw, not a sound of merriment. "He became a fat, drunken sot who despised his wife and was almost hanged by the British Government because he had the devil of a job to prove he was a privateer not a pirate."

Taylor pursed his lips. How to answer? Then he grinned. "Ah, but he had one hell of a grand funeral!"

Jesamiah snorted. "I'll look forward to that then, shall I? A funeral cortege and a wake to follow? Pity I won't be there to enjoy it."

Another silence. Both men sat staring at the haze of the distant horizon, nursing their own thoughts.

"It isn't only Tom's death, though it grieved me – I've seen enough death and injury to grow accustomed to it now. It is the regret for the past and the uncertainty of the future that trouble me," Jesamiah finally confided. "There are things..." he paused, "things I have found myself thinking about – add to that, Jennings said this futile war will soon end. What are we to do with ourselves then? Sit around kicking our heels until the next squabble between England and wherever arises? We've been pretending all this time, Malachias. You, me," he jerked his chin at the men scurrying about below on the deck, "them?"

Taylor frowned. "Pretence? I have made no pretence about loving this free life on the sea. When peace comes, not quite my taste, but we could form a mercantile business. Your head, my skill..."

Jesamiah waved him quiet, pointed, using the book as a marker. "A sail. Topgallant, four points off larb'd."

Taylor fetched his telescope from his pocket, slid it to full length and searched the horizon. "God's breath, but I wish I had your eyes, Jesamiah! You're right! Coming straight in our wake by the look of her!" He snapped the bring-it-close shut and prepared to descend via the quickest route. "Let us hope she is Spanish or French. We could do with the exercise, eh?"

"With this lack of wind?" Jesamiah answered, unenthusiastically. "English or Dutch would be better for our safety. There again," his gaze met with Taylor's, "we could attack whatever colours she's flying, whatever country her origin, could we not? It would make no difference."

Taylor frowned. "What d' you mean, lad? It could make a lot of difference." He started off down the backstay, shouting orders before his boots touched the deck.

Using the conventional way – descending by the shrouds – Jesamiah followed, taking his time to manoeuvre around the running gear and standing rigging.

A thought churning in his mind with each slow, steady, step downward.

I think, Malachias, you know well what I mean.

41

Within an hour the wind had picked up enough to billow a full spread of sail, with Captain Taylor uncertain whether to head fast for the nearest Windward Isle, or wait and see what the ship was in case she proved profitable. He opted for a middle course: a decent speed but one eye on the vessel gaining on them. Hench, made the new bosun, was the one to identify her as English Royal Navy.

"She's a bloody frigate, probably heading for Barbados."

The knowledge brought another dilemma. Head for harbour or remain innocently sauntering along? They were legal about their business, but most navy bastards had a tendency to push their weight around, especially if they needed additional crew. If the Navy demanded men – even if that meant leaving a merchant vessel woefully undermanned – then they pressed men into service without thought of a by-your-leave, recompense, or an individual's rights. On the High Seas, only the Navy had 'rights'.

Knowing *Mermaid* could not outrun nor outgun a frigate, Taylor chose the latter option. A decision he regretted when someone shouted, "She's the *Bonney Chance*."

Jesamiah looked up sharply from peering at their compass heading. "You sure, Norton?"

"As sure as hens lays eggs. Know her anywhere. I spent three years aboard before I got the opportunity to jump ship. I stayed well out the way while she was anchored at Ponti Delegardoo."

"Ponta Delgada." Frowning, Jesamiah automatically corrected the mispronunciation.

Archie Norton read the expression on his face. "I ain't the only deserter. There's ten of us who were once obliged to serve. We patrolled the coast of France and Biscay – none of the Gold Braid who knew us usually come within a gnat's piss of where we sail now. But unless she's got a new captain, that there *Bonney Chance* be a different matter. He can be a bugger, can Captain Merryat Barclay."

Taylor picked up the telescope from beside the binnacle box, brought their unwanted companion into focus and studied her. "Looks French to me," he said after a while. "Flying English colours to fool us?"

"Nay, that's the old *Bonney Chance*, alright. But you're quite right, she were *la Bonne Chance* before Barclay captured and Englishiefied 'er."

"I suggest, then," Taylor said, "that any of you who don't want to be noticed make yourself scarce below. Just in case she comes closer."

The deserters scarpered. Jesamiah hesitated.

"Something amiss?" Taylor asked.

"Only if this Captain Barclay recalls a certain incident at Ponta Delgada."

"That were long ago. Water under the bridge."

Jesamiah was not so sure, and there was the other matter to consider. But this did not seem an appropriate time to be mentioning it.

42

Bonney Chance held all the luck. The wind was with her and her captain, Barclay, as Norton had feared, was determined to set a mark of authority. _Mermaid_ was ordered to heave to so that her business could be ascertained.

"We are returning from the Africas with cargo to sell in the Caribbean Islands," Taylor said to Barclay and his first lieutenant as they stood on _Mermaid_'s heaving deck, scrutinising everything with eagle eyes. Their companion, Major General Thomas Handasyd, clung uncomfortably to a stay while attempting, unsuccessfully, to maintain his dignity as Governor of Jamaica.

Mermaid was rolling over the Atlantic swell passing under her keel, causing her to wallow like a sow in a mud-riddled pigpen. She lay there, her tight-shut gun ports on one side slipping underwater. Slowly she righted herself, was upright a brief moment, then with blocks and gear clattering and grinding she fell over to the other side, the gun tackles creaking and complaining at the excessive strain, the deck sloping so steeply it was not easy to retain a foothold. Then the process started again: roll, dip, roll.

"We carry timber, silver, pewter and Dutch china tableware," Taylor explained, hanging on to a belaying pin to keep his balance, a false congenial smile to his countenance.

"Nice stuff, blue and white Delftware porcelain. A nice gift for your good lady wife, perhaps?"

"You came by these goods honestly?" Barclay queried, making no comment about a lady wife. "We recently encountered the wreckage of a trader."

Taylor answered with honesty. "Nothing to do with us, I assure you." It was the truth. Everything they attacked left no trace – was burned or went to the bottom of the ocean.

"You are a privateer?" the lieutenant piped up. He gestured to the crew and guns.

"Aye," Taylor answered, "if opportunity and circumstances conjoin, but for this voyage I carry only mercantile goods. Our armament is for defence. We are at war with Spain, you know."

Heading without invitation towards Taylor's Great Cabin, Barclay announced, "I will inspect your ledgers."

The arrogance was an affront, but no one argued with the Royal Navy, although Governor Handasyd had the decency to appear embarrassed.

"Acorne here will make everything available," Taylor responded with a tight smile, gesturing casually towards his cabin to make the intrusion appear cordial. Knucklebone Jake was prudently absent, hidden with the other deserters deep in the hold.

"You have had a profitable cruise, Captain Taylor?" Handasyd asked. "I trust our disagreement a few months ago at Port Royal is forgotten?"

"I do not even recall it," Taylor answered with a bow. He did, of course. Recalled it very well, but the business of additional tax on goods, which were, essentially, contraband was not a suitable topic of conversation.

Polite, Taylor remarked, "What sees you aboard a Royal Navy frigate, Governor?"

"I have been to England – my health, you know. I voyage to Barbados as Barclay's guest, and from there, another vessel to Jamaica. Possibly my last year. I am soon to retire."

"I am sorry to hear that," Taylor answered as he held his cabin door open. He spoke truthfully. Despite extra tax,

Handasyd's loss would be great. Governors willing to bend rules were few and far between.

Jesamiah placed various documents before Barclay, who, seated at Taylor's table, peered at neat columns of figures and handwriting.

"Here…and here…" Captain Barclay said, tapping his finger at two random entries.

"Legitimate trade. But there is nothing illegal about privateering against Queen Anne's enemies," Taylor answered, hiding his anxiety.

"That there is not," Barclay responded, "although, there is a difference between privateering and piracy. We cannot have a free-for-all. You carry a Letter of Marque?"

The moment Taylor had dreaded. He cleared his throat noisily. "I am ashamed to admit that it has become lost—" he started, but Jesamiah, shuffling through various papers, interrupted and produced a tattered piece of parchment.

"I located it, Captain, caught between some old invoices." He smiled, gave it to Barclay, who scrutinised it for several minutes, then handed it to Governor Handasyd who was busy studying the wooden figurehead.

"Eh? What's this?"

"Our Letter of Marque," Jesamiah said.

The governor frowned, repeated, "Letter of Marque?"

"Aye. Letter of Marque. That is your signature, is it not?" Barclay barked.

Handasyd studied the parchment through squinting eyes. "Without my eye-glass…" he peered closer, nodded and passed the document back to Jesamiah. "I believe it is my hand, aye."

"Are you not certain?"

Handasyd stifled irritation. "I am not, Captain Barclay, in the habit of having my word questioned."

Barclay grunted but made no apology. "All seems to be in order. Mind you keep it so, Taylor." He took up his hat and returned to the deck where his lieutenant was waiting.

"Captain, one of our escort," Lieutenant Vance indicated a

seaman, "recognises that fellow." He pointed to Jesamiah. "Speak up, Buckeridge, tell Captain Barclay what you told me."

Buckeridge whipped off his woollen cap, saluted, said smartly, "I recognise this man, sir. He was the one who murdered five of our men at Ponta Delgado."

Jesamiah's stomach somersaulted. This man couldn't possibly…could he?

"On what grounds," Taylor asked, annoyed, "do you make such an accusation? If I recall, that disgraceful deed took place at night. Those Portuguese have no liking for efficient street illumination."

"There was light enough for me to see that gold acorn earring of his!"

"You are certain of this, Buckeridge?" Barclay queried.

"As certain as I am standing here, Cap'n."

"Well then," Jesamiah answered with a small bow and a wide smile, "you have the wrong man." He twiddled the earring between his finger and thumb. "I took this off a sea-snake called Charles Vane some months ago in lieu of a debt he owes me. Partial payment." He broadened his smile with the plausible lie. "I would be obliged, Captain Barclay, should you encounter Vane, to obtain fifty guineas on my behalf before you hang him."

Unconvinced, Lieutenant Vance asked Buckeridge, "Did you see the murderer's face?"

"No, sir, just the earring. It's a design to easily recognise again I'd say."

"Like I said," Jesamiah insisted, "had I known Vane was wanted for murder, I would have reconsidered my options, and taken some other token…alas…"

"False accusation, Captain Barclay, is a serious business," Taylor stated with authority. "If we can continue our voyage without further hindrance…?"

Outmanoeuvred, Barclay conceded defeat. "Very well, but while here, I am short-handed. I need a dozen of your men."

"Begging pardon, Captain, that is not acceptable. My men are required for the merchant trade…"

Barclay placed his hand on the sword at his hip. "You have more than adequate crew. Lieutenant, select twelve men."

Taylor appealed to Governor Handasyd, who spread his hands and regretfully shook his head. What could Taylor do except quietly fume as eleven of his men were forcibly taken to serve Queen Anne?

For the twelfth, the lieutenant motioned towards Jesamiah. "You. You will suffice for us."

A series of emotions coursed through Jesamiah, ranging from disbelief to anger.

However, Barclay growled a countermand. "Not him, he has the manner of a troublemaker about him."

"I can lick discipline into him, sir."

"That you might, Lieutenant, but I have no fancy for potential mutineers aboard my ship. Select another."

Barclay, gesturing for Governor Handasyd to precede him, descended the ladder cleats to the gig below.

"I know it were you," Buckeridge sneered at Jesamiah. "Them were my mates. Mark me, I will have revenge."

"Duly marked," Jesamiah retorted. "I look forward to seeing you try."

"THAT WAS CLOSE," Taylor said, relieved, as *Bonney Chance* showed them her stern. "There was nothing I could do for those men – had I tried, he may have searched us for deserters. Or illicit cargo."

"The latter of which he would not have found," Jesamiah snapped, angry beyond words. "He had no way of discovering that our ledgers are false. I've seen to that. You should not have let him take those men. However, it is done and the wind is rising. Do we get under way?"

Taylor stared at him through narrowed eyes. "Aye, we do, then come to my cabin. I want a word."

Curt, Jesamiah nodded. "Aye. Sir."

43

"Explain."

Taylor's single, angry, word was terse as an hour later Jesamiah ambled into the Great Cabin – he had deliberately not hurried. He removed his hat, placed it on the table, and with only the rise of one questioning eyebrow for permission, poured himself a generous glass of brandy. He went to the chair next to Taylor, sat, crossed his legs and sipped the liquor.

"Mmm, good stuff. Is this the last of what we took off that Frenchie? The wind's strengthening. Storm clouds building. We could be in for a blow."

Taylor leant forward, his brows dipping downward. "Fok the wind and the clouds. I said, explain."

"Funnily enough," Jesamiah answered, looking straight at him, "I was going to ask you the same."

Fury rising, Taylor leapt from his chair, knocking it over, and slammed his fist on the table. "You try my patience at times, Master Jesamiah Acorne. Explain yourself, sir, before I really lose my temper!"

Downing the brandy with one gulp, Jesamiah also got to his feet. He jabbed his finger into Taylor's sternum. "I have saved you and this entire crew from the noose. Be grateful for it."

"Grateful? For what? For you making a damn fool of me!"

Jesamiah grasped the lace cravat at Taylor's throat. He was taller than Malachias now, and had developed confidence in

147

himself. Nostrils flaring to match Taylor's anger, he thrust his face closer to his captain's.

"You," he said, giving a small shake with each word, "are angry because your deliberate falsehood has been uncovered. I forged that Letter of Marque for you. That alone deserves a generous thank you, but just when were you thinking of admitting that *Mermaid* has not sailed under a genuine document since King Billy popped his Dutch clogs?" He pushed Taylor away with such force that the man staggered and collapsed onto Jesamiah's vacated chair.

Righting the overturned one, then refilling his glass, Jesamiah poured another drink for Taylor. Grim-faced, handed it to him, took several deep breaths to calm his boiling temper. "When were you going to tell the truth, Malachias? That we are sea-wolf pirates?"

Taylor stared back at Jesamiah, his own rage subsiding, seeing Charles Mereno, Jesamiah's father, so clearly in not just the lad's features, but the way he stood and spoke; the way he *thought*. Charles had been a good friend – no, more like a brother – they'd saved each other's lives on more than one occasion, aye and argued and fallen out on as many more. Made up again over a keg of rum. They had trusted each other, a trust that had gone beyond question or condition. Could the lad also be trusted? Even if he could, was he *worth* trusting? A man could stand at your back in a fight and fight with you. Or he could stand there, useless, do nothing but piss himself. Just how much like his father *was* this young lad? Quick to laugh, formidable when angry?

Taylor cocked his head to one side. "Would it make a difference if I told you that your father had, technically, been a pirate, not a privateer?"

"No. It wouldn't." Jesamiah swallowed a mouthful of brandy, topped up his glass from the depleted bottle.

Mermaid's Captain sat back in his chair. Straightforward plain speaking; another trait of Charles Mereno's; he'd never stood for nonsense, nor suffered fools. Taylor regarded the lad opposite him through assessing eyes, sipped his brandy. Lad? Nay, he was almost a man now, for all that he was, what?

Sixteen? Seventeen? Taylor suppressed a snort. Whatever age he was, he'd not been honest about it.

"I respected your father, Jes. Still do."

"Do you? I don't. I never did, never will."

Taylor tried again. "Look lad, he had his reasons for being, shall we say, distant, from you." He had no idea if what he'd just said was true or not. What he did know, Charles had been proud of his youngest son. But had he wanted him to follow in his wake? Face the probability of the hangman's noose? Did a father want that for a son?

Taking his time to think, Taylor sipped again at his drink – to think on what to think, and to think on what to say. If Jesamiah were his own son... Ah, if Jesamiah were his own he'd be proud to have him here, by his side – as a privateer *or* a pirate. Did it matter which? There was a fine line between the two anyway. A very fine line. Did the lad understand that?

"Morgan, Drake, Raleigh, they all professed to be privateers," he said with a shrug, then laughed. "They weren't, least, not to the Spanish they weren't."

When Jesamiah made no answer he added, "Old Halyard Calpin told you to find me. We did a lot together, the three of us. Lived, laughed, fucked, faced death. Halyard would have known what he was sending you to. A life at sea; a life of freedom." He leant forward resting his arm on his thigh. How to handle this anger that was rubbing within the boy? An anger directed at his disappointment in his father more than anything. Angry resentment that was distorting his judgement of other things. Should he shout at the lad to make him see sense? Goad, sneer, reprimand? Make excuses? Placate with pretty words? Or tell the plain truth and have done with it.

Taylor shook his head, sighed, then half-smiled. "You really don't realise how much you are like him, do you?"

Jesamiah was about to answer – something disparaging by the crumpling of his eyes and mouth – but Taylor held up a hand to silence him. "One day you'll appreciate your father. Who he was what he did, and why he did it, but at the moment you're letting your childhood eat you alive. You are no longer that snivelling brat blaming your absent pa for everything that went wrong. Get over it. Sail on. Calpin sent you to me because he knew this would be the best place for you. At sea. The sea's in your blood, like me, like your father..."

The retort came sharp.

"I keep telling you, I'm not like my father!"

The impatience rose in Taylor, spilled over. He shouted. "Well that's where you're fokin' wrong, boy! Your father was a belligerent, mule-headed, stubborn bugger – just like you are being right this very moment. But he was also a damn fine man, the finest I knew, an' because I loved him like a brother, I love you like a son!"

There! He'd said it! "I don't care a gnat's fart for this bloody great anchor of self-pity that you carry around with you. But what I *do* care about, is seeing you mature into a bloody fine seaman. The best there is because your father before you was the best, and the best stay alive."

For several minutes Jesamiah glared back at the older man, was tempted to point out that his father was dead, but he let the sarcasm go, that wasn't what Taylor had meant.

Taylor rose from his chair, brandy glass still in his hand, went to gaze out of the stern windows. Their wake was good and strong, and straight. Jesamiah had been right, though, he noted, storm clouds were building up.

Were sons obliged to grow up to be like their fathers? He thought of his own, a man he barely knew because at ten years old he'd escaped the brute by running away to sea. He turned back to look at Jesamiah, sitting there, saying nothing, face expressionless.

"Decide what it is that *you* want, Jes. What *you* want to do, where *you* want to go, what *you* want to be. I'll not stop you. Though I admit I'll be sorry were you to decide to head ashore."

"I don't have to go ashore," Jesamiah answered, that touch of belligerence returning. "I could join the Navy."

Taylor pursed his lips, nodded slowly. "Aye, that you could. In time you might become a captain, and maybe Queen Anne'll grant you a Letter of Marque to hunt pirates." He sighed, expelling air out through puffed cheeks. "Pirates or privateers, lad, it don't make much difference. What makes the difference is being good at what we do. If you inform on us, we, all of us, will hang."

"I have no intention of informing!" Jesamiah retorted, hurt that Taylor could think such a betrayal of him. Admitted, "It isn't the act, Malachias, it's the deceit. If I'm going to hang one day in the future, I'd rather know why they're putting a noose round my neck and pushing me off a barrel. I assume this is why Handasyd wanted a higher percentage of the profit back in Port Royal those months ago?"

Relieved that the anger had dissipated – hah! Charles had always been just as quick to haul from one mood to another! – Taylor nodded, "Aye, he was as worried as I when Barclay asked to see our papers. If I hang, he'll see the end of easy money, and his name blackened to boot."

Jesamiah spread his hands. "Then why not grant you a legal document?"

"And kiss goodbye to extra commission? Nay, while it suits them, these sort of people like to keep us roped over a barrel"

Jesamiah thought on that, nodded. That made sense. Uncomfortable sense, but sense all the same. He shrugged. "The men ought to know the truth though, don't you think?"

Captain Taylor wiped his hand across his nose. Charles Mereno had always harboured fair play and truth. What was right for one was right for another. But he had also been shrewd, and knew the sense of, well, being sensible where his own neck was concerned. Sense was shouting that Jesamiah was right, damn him, but Taylor knew that he'd buggered up and did not want to tell it to his crew. That would give them the right to elect another captain. And he had no intention of taking that risk.

Taylor sniffed, studied his feet a moment, then stared Jesamiah straight in the eye. "And will you be telling them?"

Jesamiah stood up, put his empty glass on the table, set his hat on his head and walked to the door.

"I'll think on it."

44

The dreams came again, trembling through Jesamiah's sleep, waking him with a start, his heart pounding. Had he cried out? If he had, no one paid heed – they were all too dead to the world with tiredness.

The wind had strengthened to a storm that had battered them without mercy for five days. The topgallant mast had snapped, the mainsail had shredded beyond repair. Running on bare poles, the helmsman lashed to the wheel, lifelines set fore and aft, the noise of the wind and the angry sea, coupled with the groans of the ship, had drowned all but the nearest shouts.

Three men had died: two falling from the mainmast to the deck; one washed overboard. There had been no hope of rescuing him.

The dreams were of the Cornish girl, her dark eyes wide with terror, and her concern for his safety evident.

Every moment of exhausted, snatched sleep during those days of storm-lashed tempest her face had been there, in his mind. Even with the storm waning, the men had struggled to keep awake, attending to essential repairs as best they could: jury-rigging, splicing, binding, mending, replacing. With barely opened, red-rimmed eyes, drenched through, his hands as stiff and sore as his body, Jesamiah had worked automatically, only partially aware that the girl's ethereal presence was keeping him safe.

Finally came the opportunity to roll into the nearest hammock and fall instantly asleep; a gratitude that had vanished as he lay there one hour later staring into the swaying darkness. Even awake, he could see her face. Who was she? Who *was* she!

___

45

CORNWALL

Tiola heard her father shouting her name but ignored him. She would receive a whipping for not attending evening church, but there were more important things for her to be about this day. The young man needed her attention, for his ship, his life, was in danger. God would understand. Although her father would not.

Mama had said that the child was ill, was to remain abed, but Papa had gainsaid her, slammed into her room and demanded she rise and dress herself. Tiola had looked at him, blank, pale-faced, unblinking.

~ *Go away!* ~ The words had been in her mind, not spoken aloud, but still he had turned around and gone away.

How did I do that? she wondered, but noted the doing as the door closed and his footsteps sounded on the wooden stairs as he descended.

He shouted again from the parlour, then she heard the front door of the house open and the bustle of them all leaving. The crunch of their feet on the gravel path outside. The house settled into silence, only Tompkin, the black and white cat, curled at the bottom of her bed purred in contentment.

Tiola smiled, returned her attention to the painting of the ship that hung on her wall. It was a brig under full sail, churning her way through a choppy sea, with scudding clouds racing across a blue, blue sky above her. But Tiola did not see the waves. Or the clouds or the sky, all she saw was a storm lashing rain and a wind howling its temper, and the black-haired young man struggling to stay alive.

"Keep safe," she muttered, then sent the words to him through her mind.

~ *Keep safe!* ~

46

BARBADOS

"What do you intend to do?" Taylor asked outright that first evening when conditions had calmed to something more reasonable, although the wind was still gusting and the sea tossed rougher than a whore's bad-mouthed temper.

Barbados was an hour ahead at most. They would be making anchorage after dark, but that suited well because *Bonney Chance* could be there. The plan was to reprovision with essentials only and be on their way with the next tide, before too many realised they had come and gone. Even so, the men were chattering eagerly about making landfall. Barbados, being English-held, was always a favourite. Several of the crew intended to stay ashore – the sea called to adventure for a while, but wives and sweethearts often won out in the end.

Jesamiah was at the helm, gentling the spokes to keep *Mermaid* on their designated compass heading. He was not so enthusiastic about their destination. Barbados was sugar-cane country, the land owned by rich merchants and farmed by black slaves. He had no taste for rich merchants or slavery.

A last gust from the storm staggered *Mermaid*, sending a stream of white water along her lee rail. He let her pay off until the flurry passed by, then brought her back. The wind whipped at his hair and blue ribbons, tendrils batting at his cheek as he guided *Mermaid* closer to the wind – the main topgallant shivered, and smiling, Jesamiah eased his grip. He had her where he wanted her.

"I said," Taylor repeated, his arms folded, "what do you intend to do?"

"About what?" Jesamiah responded as he looked along the deck beyond the spread of sail to the men scurrying about. He enjoyed these rare-given chances to take the helm whenever they were offered.

"You know what."

Glancing at Taylor, Jesamiah shrugged. Beyond staying alive during the storm where one slip of concentration could have caused a different, more fatal slip, he'd not had any opportunity to think about other things.

"I reckon I can either go against you or stay with you."

"And…?" Malachias Taylor prompted.

Jesamiah took one hand off the helm and fiddled with his earring. He was in no hurry to ease away any of the man's anxiety. He looked at Taylor, then back to the sails. "Governors such as Handasyd will not be so tolerant when this war is over. When convenient excuses are removed and documents revealed as forgeries, privateering will cease, and there will only be piracy left."

"But we are still at war. It will not happen yet."

"Are you so sure of that?" Raising his head a little, Jesamiah squinted through narrowed eyes out to sea. "Who's on watch?"

"Beratt."

Jesamiah scowled. "Beratt? He's probably sound asleep. Take a look over there." He pointed. "We've got company."

Taylor cursed and snapped open his spyglass just as Hench, fastening his breeches, called out in alarm from the heads.

"Cap'n! Company! Unfriendly, by the look of it." He indicated a puff of smoke, which was followed by the distant *whoomph* of sound. Cannon.

Muttering a lewd word, Taylor snarled, "It's the *Jamaica Rose*. I'd know her anywhere."

Jesamiah also swore, the habit picked up from Malachias. "What the fok is she doing out here? She's the Jamaican guardship, she has no business near Barbados."

Hench had trotted the length of the deck and stood nearby, joined by several more of the crew, all staring gape-mouthed as the *Jamaica Rose* fired a second warning – much too far away to be any danger, but her meaning was plain.

"Only a guess," Hench said, spitting a wedge of saliva-drenched tobacco over the side, "but I reckon she's lookin' fer us."

Taylor's jaw was set as tight as his balled fists. "Handasyd mentioned something... I wager he made arrangements for her to meet him at Barbados."

"And she is captained by our friend Stannis," Jesamiah added, as casually as if remarking about a sunny day.

"Who is probably still annoyed that we stuffed him good an' proper," Knucklebone Jake agreed.

Jesamiah brought *Mermaid* up closer into the wind to adjust for a rainsquall that was flurrying past. Said, "Do we surrender, fight, or run like smoke and oakum and hope to lose the bastard once night falls?"

The men gathering along the rails muttered between themselves. None had a view to surrender, but water was low. "If we run, she will only come after us again," Norton announced. Muttered agreements following.

"Should've stayed t'other side of the Pond," someone else remarked.

"You were a bloody fool, Taylor," another man grumbled, although whether he meant their location or the cause of the situation, was unclear. "You've put us all in danger."

Shouts of "Aye" and "We need a new captain!" were accompanied by raised fists. Anger fuelled by building fear.

"Arguing will not solve our predicament," Jesamiah pointed out, handing the helm to O'Bartlett. "We can do the shit-slinging later."

Taylor tossed him a grateful glance. "I know these waters. If we run along the coast there's a cove with a good water supply..."

"Oh aye?" Norton mocked. "We drop anchor and then find ourselves trapped?"

Taylor kept his patience and temper. "Allow me to finish.

Stannis will guess we need fresh water. We make him *think* we are heading for the cove, get him to chase us, then veer off below the headland. There are shoals, rocks and sandbanks there, a depth and channel clear enough for *Mermaid* but risky for the *Jamaica Rose*. They'll not be able to follow."

Jesamiah felt the need to state a fact. "We will be regarded as hostile to an English vessel. Which will mean," he looked significantly at Taylor, then from man to man, "that we will be marked as pirates."

"Been that for a long time, lad," O'Bartlett said as he adjusted the helm.

"We are privateers," Taylor countered.

O'Bartlett answered with a casual shrug of indifference. "So you 'ave kept sayin' these Gawd knows 'ow many years, Cap'n. Not one of us 'as ever believed it."

At the incredulous expression on Taylor's face, Jesamiah roared with laughter. "That's well an' truly scuppered m'protests of fancy indignation then, ain't it? Seems I can't make no complaint – I've been sailin' as a pirate all along!" He clapped his friend, Malachias Taylor, on the shoulder. "I guess, in the long run, it don't really make much difference, do it? "

47

Starlight was scattered across the sky above and reflected in the sea below. A rising three-quarter moon cast her light in a path of silvered gold. The occasional flurry of rain darted across the night. Spray tossed over *Mermaid*'s bow and water creamed along her hull as she ran closer in towards the surf-ruffled, rocky Barbados shore. Dogged, the *Jamaica Rose* lumbered less than two miles in her wake, the moon too bright to offer concealment for either vessel.

Hovering near Malachias on the quarterdeck, Jesamiah felt uneasy. They would have to shorten more sail soon – it was all very well Taylor saying he knew these waters, but a gusting wind and a jagged shore were not friends to sailors. And he could hear her – the mermaid. Her sweet, alluring voice singing so beautifully. He closed his ears to the sound by concentrating on the white surf and the silhouetted headland reaching towards the larboard bow, appearing, although still distant, as if it were about to loom alongside.

"Take in t'gallant," Taylor ordered. "O'Bartlett, bring her up two points larboard."

"Two points larb'd," O'Bartlett echoed.

Jesamiah clenched his fingers around the nearest rail. The main course was already clewed up, guns ready to run out, gun crews eager while apprehensive. *Jamaica Rose* was larger and carried more crew, more guns, but she was not as agile, her men not as experienced. Nor had they that edge of determination to stay alive.

"We'll be close in if the wind veers," Jesamiah observed.

In reply, Taylor shouted, "Man the braces!"

O'Bartlett spun the spokes of the helm, squinting through the moon-bright night at the flapping canvas and the tilt of the compass in the binnacle box. Yet another flurry of wind and rain sped across the starboard quarter before hurtling off to harry the *Jamaica Rose* instead.

~ Come. Make love to me…~

"Do you think there are such things as mermaids?" Jesamiah asked, to no one in particular.

"If there are," O'Bartlett answered, "those rocks ahead'll be where they lurk, luring in ship an' sailor alike."

His answer was not reassuring.

Spray lifted across the weather rail, drenching Jesamiah. He paid no heed. The headland was waiting to snatch them up, at its base the surf was bubbling and hissing like a brew in a witch's cauldron.

"Leadsman to the chains, if you please, Mr Acorne," Taylor said as calmly as if he were ordering afternoon tea for a lady.

"I've already sent someone," Jesamiah responded.

On cue, Tab hollered, "By the mark six!"

More than enough water for *Mermaid*.

"By the mark five!"

A *whoomph*, a flare of light, then another. *Jamaica Rose* was altering course; aware of the sea danger ahead, was firing her guns as she passed astern, aiming for *Mermaid*'s vulnerable rear. Instinctively, Jesamiah ducked as the first and second *whish* of grapeshot and langrage hurtled into the transom and slashed along the open deck, gouging splinters as the barrage passed through. Three men, injured, cried out; a fourth, his shout of agony abruptly ended as grapeshot tore into his throat, killing him straight out.

"Deep four!" Tab shouted, ignoring what was happening.

There was nothing *Mermaid* could do except keep to her course; she was shuddering and bucking as turbulence swept beneath her hull. But the *Jamaica Rose* had not finished yet, as each of her guns came to bear, she was firing as if her existence depended upon it. *Mermaid*'s rigging pinged as it snapped, wood cracked and boomed, the Great Cabin's glass windows shattered as shot after shot gouged into the stern. How the rudder was not damaged was a miracle. Then *Mermaid* slewed off course. Taylor, blood streaming from his cheek and hands, ran to grasp the helm as O'Bartlett fell, blood pouring from a shattered arm, half of which was no longer there. Men ran as lithe as athletes, not needing orders to keep *Mermaid* in check, to keep her as near they could on course. Damaged rigging was hacked away, braces and yards squealed, she bumped and kicked. A scraping sound.

"Rudder's not responding!" Taylor shouted. "We're aground!"

Jesamiah ran to the taffrail and peered down into the black sea.

"Sandbank!" he yelled. "Looks like the rudder's stuck!"

A quarter of a mile distant, aware of the rocks, the *Jamaica Rose* was slowly turning away, making ready to present her larboard battery and another rolling broadside of guns.

48

"We've got to lighten her aft!" Jesamiah yelled as he ran to Malachias' cabin, men who needed no second telling joining him. Inside, the mess was indescribable. What could be broken was broken, debris was strewn everywhere. No more salt-rimed transom windows, merely a great, gaping hole as wide as a scream. Men started tossing furniture out through it, but Jesamiah yelled at them to belay.

"Just this," he roared. "The bloody figurehead's weighing us down." The proud painted man had fallen, the supporting tethers severed, part of its right side smashed. "Quick! You and you, jury-rig a hoist. God alone knows how we'll manage to heave it out."

Seamen acted silently, quickly; years of experience in working with rope, cordage, pulley and hoist coming into use. Jesamiah glanced out across the moonlit sea to beyond the white churn of surf.

"Thank God," he muttered, relieved as the incompetents aboard the *Jamaica Rose* missed stays, their turn a shambles – but a shambles that would not last long.

"Come on…! Two…six…heave! Two…six…heave…!"

The bloody thing would not budge. The wooden face, so like his father's, stared up at Jesamiah as if mocking him.

~ I let you down, but I have always loved you, son. Believe that I have…~

Jesamiah did not want to hear. He had no particular love for his father, and needed none in return. He peered through the gaping hole that was once the stern, the *Jamaica Rose* at the edge of his vision, her bodged turn almost completed – a broadside was moments away. Swept along by the gusting wind, another curtain of rain passed through the moon's bright shaft of light slanting across the sea. The same gust caught the *Jamaica Rose*. Unbalanced, she veered and heeled over as if a petulant child had kicked at an unwanted toy.

"She'll not claw off in time!" Jesamiah shouted, the rope grasped in his hand as he stared in fascinated horror at the churning surf stretching out from the headland, reaching out like snarling fingers to gras their prey. "She's done for!"

They stopped hauling at the figurehead and peered out into the rain-misted moonlit dark, relieved for themselves, aghast as the other ship careered towards her certain death.

The cracking, grinding and splintering howled through the night as the *Jamaica Rose* slewed sideways onto the rocks. Her foremast swayed, broke, fell, her rigging snapping, canvas tearing and crumpling as if it were made of paper. The length of her hull split with a rendering crash – she rolled over and went down, her keel torn away, water flooding in. Her men drowned before they even knew what had happened. Some, a few only, had jumped clear, their cries for help vying with the mermaid's lilting song of destruction as she called their souls to her side.

~ Come! Come to me! ~

"I've no regard for Stannis, but we ought to help," Jesamiah cried. "Send a boat across!"

"Nay, unless they can swim, they're done for. We need to see to our own salvation, not theirs!"

As if agreeing, as if some spiritual force had intervened in their plight, *Mermaid* rolled slightly, and the figurehead moved. Carried by its own weight and momentum, it slid forward towards what was left of the shattered window frames. A moment of silence, then cheering as the great, lumbering thing slithered out into the night, the stricken *Jamaica Rose* forgotten. The weight gone, *Mermaid* floated free of the sandbank, but Jesamiah could still hear her, the other mermaid, calling.

~ *Come! Come to me!* ~

Still connected, the great length of rope snaked out after the figurehead, writhing and twisting as it ran. Shouting a warning, those men clutching it let go, but it curled, snagged, caught around Jesamiah's wrist, and unable to free himself, took him with it.

~ *Come to me! Come to me!* ~

49

———

Cold. So bloody cold! Down and down Jesamiah went, unable to see or hear anything beyond the rush of water and the pounding beat of his heart drumming in his ears. One-handed, he tried to loosen the loop around his wrist, but it only pulled tighter. Down and down into the cold darkness where no moon, star or sunlight penetrated… Then arms were around him, a face before his, black hair, dark eyes; incongruously, a smell of wild flowers and hay meadows flooded his senses.

~ *Do not struggle. Let me help.* ~ The Cornish girl.

Everything stilled. The lack of air crushing his lungs eased, the rushing sound in his ears quietened. It was as if someone else was breathing for him.

His wrist ached abominably, the wet rope squeezing tighter and tighter – then, suddenly, it snapped. He was free! He clawed upward. Moonlight! Starlight! His head broke through the surface, the sea around frothing, churning and buffeting. He gasped for air, coughing and spluttering. His foot kicked something solid; desperate, he grappled at what he took to be floating debris, and almost sobbed aloud when he looked straight into the painted eyes of the partially submerged figurehead floating beside him.

The low-hanging moon shone bright; the rain was skimming across the sea; hurrying before it, a scatter of droplets driven by the wind. Jesamiah stretched out his arms, the better to float, the

166

frayed end of the rope, still entwined around his wrist, dangling. And for a matter of moments only, appearing across the sky in front of him was the perfect arc of a glorious, white moonbow, and caught in its soft, silver-gold light, the mermaid sat perched atop the wooden figurehead, her hands lovingly caressing the carved features which looked so like the human she had once loved.

~ You came! You came back to me! ~

Salt tears of joy trickled down her cheeks as moonlight shimmered on the droplets of her wet hair, glistened on her naked shoulders and breasts and illuminated the scales of her fish's tail, creating dancing sparkles of jewel-like colours.

She looked up, saw Jesamiah, and smiled.

~ Thank you. ~

Jesamiah nodded back at her. Thought the words: *~ It is the best I can do for you. ~*

~ It is enough, my son. It is enough. ~

And then she sang, her words meaningless to his ears, but her voice was the sound of the sea, the hush of the waves, the breath of the tides; timeless, ethereal and beautiful, lifting and soaring to meet the watching stars and the fading light of the moonbow. Its very tip, the last of the celestial light to vanish, piercing downward into the black sea where the figurehead, saturated by water, was slowly sinking.

The other end of the rope, still tangled around Jesamiah's wrist, jerked, he grabbed hold of its sodden length with his other hand and, like a fish hooked to a line, felt himself being hauled towards his ship. He glanced back, once, the salt water stinging his eyes, spewing into his nostrils and mouth, fancied he saw a fish's tail disappear beneath the waves.

Bruised, battered and shivering, he slumped on the floor of Captain Taylor's cabin, gasping for breath, fending off the desire to vomit and the patting hands of his friends as they thumped his back and shoulders. On deck, Taylor was hollering for the injured to be tended and this bloody mess to be cleared up.

50

DECEMBER 4TH 1710

A new, replacement *Mermaid* dozed at her anchor cable, while her captain and crew lazed around a blazing fire built on the beach. Tomorrow – or if they were not sober enough, the next day – they intended to sail for Nassau where pirates were made welcome, plunder was traded for silver and gold, and questions were never asked.

Falling on the luck of encountering a Spanish merchant brig within three days of their encounter with the *Jamaica Rose*, the Mermaids had commandeered her with ease by hoisting Spanish colours, and Jesamiah making use of his knowledge of the language again. They disposed of the crew, salvaged all they could from the stricken soon-to-be abandoned old *Mermaid* and made the necessary alterations to their new vessel in the secrecy of this secluded cove. Gun ports to be fitted, rigging to be altered, the precious mermaid figurehead to set in place, proud, at the bow, and the Spanish name across the stern painted out, the new one painted in. Pirates had a dislike for renaming a vessel, it brought bad luck, but Malachias maintained that to keep the same name kept the bad luck at bay.

"She might look, handle, sail, different but *Mermaid* is *Mermaid*, her soul is in her figurehead and her name. That's all that counts."

They had not hurried to complete the work. The inhabitants had fled in fear of their lives to the forest. The island had water, fowl and wild pigs; the Spaniard's hold had supplied other necessities, including kegs of decent rum and brandy.

In the days of hard, but pleasurable work, Jesamiah had forgotten all about the mermaid, his father's voice – and the Cornish girl.

Tiola watched him from the sanctuary of the hay barn, her father safe away tending a sick man in Truro, although she and her mother knew there was no sickness, nor was the 'patient' a man.

Her Craft was awakening, but was not yet ready to blossom into full strength. She had enough knowledge, though, to wisely step away from the handsome young man with the black, curly hair, the blue ribbons laced into it and the gold acorn dangling from his ear – for now.

~ *Until it is the right time, you will not remember me,* ~ she whispered into his mind as he sprawled, drunk, on the beach, drowsing beneath a sky full of stars.

~ *And you will forget her, the Lorelei, forever.* ~

HE STARED up at the stars, seeing a blur of twice as many as there actually were, lay, giggling to himself.

Today was his seventeenth birthday, and he was so content, so inebriated, that he fancied he could hear the sea talking to him in a *swi…shh…shsshh* sound as the waves rushed in, spilled, then retreated again over the shingle…

~ *Jesshh…a…miah. Jesshh…a…miah…*~

~ DROP ANCHOR ~

AUTHOR'S NOTE

History does not always fit neatly into fiction, particularly where characters are concerned. Some of the names in my story are factual people, others are fictional: Henry Jennings, Charles Vane and Major General Handasyd, Governor of Jamaica were real. Vane, a notoriously vicious and cruel pirate, was eventually hanged. Jennings was a privateer who captained *Barsheba*. He is one of the few who retired honourably, and often appears in the *Sea Witch Voyages* – usually to Jesamiah's dismay. Mayor Smallwood, most of the other characters, and, alas, Jesamiah himself are my own creations.

Factually, England was at war with Spain, and Letters of Marque were issued as a 'licence to kill'. Without one, you could be hanged for piracy. Henry Morgan is fact, as is the 1692 earthquake. Recent underwater archaeology has identified the remains of what was known as The Wickedest City in the World. It has always been believed that a tsunami after the earthquake wiped the city out, but recent evidence suggests a shifting of the tectonic plates, which dropped the level of the land and left substantial ruins submerged. Many governors of these colonies, remote from England, were corrupt, taking a vast percentage of the privateers' (and pirates'!) loot for themselves. There is no evidence that Governor Handasyd was one of them, though.

The legend of Lorelei is an old one, although mostly associated with the River Rhine and the Lorelei Rock, but I thought it would be fun to give the River Siren a different existence. As for Tethys, the Spirit of the Sea, she is very briefly mentioned here in this tale, but has her own part to play in the *Sea Witch Voyages* and Jesamiah's life.

Mermaids, of course, do not exist, and neither do Cornish girls who turn out to be white witches – but Jesamiah is destined to be reunited with Tiola…

As for moonbows, they occur when the moon is at the right height and rain is in the air. They are rare, but a few sailors *have* seen one.

My thanks to Nicky, the late Richard Tearle and Caz for

reading through various draft versions, and to Cathy Helms of www.avalongraphics.org for the beautiful cover and for formatting the text of this edition.

Finally, thank you to all Jesamiah's fans for your enthusiasm and support. Jes and I very much appreciate it.

Helen Hollick, 2021

https://www.helenhollick.net

EXCERPT - SEA WITCH

THE FIRST VOYAGE OF CAPTAIN JESAMIAH ACORNE

Beware of Pirates, for danger lurks behind their smiles…

IN THE DEPTHS, in the abyss of darkness at the very bottom of the oceans, Tethys stirred.

She was the Soul of the sea, the Spirit of the waves, and was capable, as the mood took her, of benign complaisance or malicious rage. She was without form or solidity, yet she saw, heard and became aware of everything within her jurisdiction. She ruled her water realm with unchallenged power, and a terrible omnipotence.

ONE: Late January - 1716

Mermaid was moving fast, the ship bowling along with her sails filled, the canvas billowing, cordage creaking and straining. She climbed over the next wave, her bow lifting to linger a moment before swooping down into another deluge of spray. Completing the seesaw movement, her stern soared high as the roller trundled beneath her keel. The wind smelt of hot, dry and dusty land, of jungle and grass savannah. Of Africa.

The lookout, clad in an old shirt and sailor's breeches was perched high in the crosstrees, one hundred and thirty feet above the deck. Excited, he pointed to the horizon. "Over there, Jesamiah, that's where I saw 'er. I swear I saw a sail!"

With the ease of years of practice, Jesamiah Acorne stepped from the rigging on to the narrow platform that swayed with the lift and plunge of the ship. He hooked his arm through a t'gallant shroud, brought his telescope to his eye, and scanned the ocean. Nothing. Nothing except a flat expanse of blue emptiness going on, unbroken, for twenty miles. And beyond that? Another twenty, and another.

These were the waters of the Gulf of Guinea, the huge stretch of sea beneath the bulb of land where the trade wealth of West Africa was turned into fat profit: gold, ivory and slaves. The African coast, where merchants found their plentiful supply of human misery and where an entire ships' crew could be wiped out by fever within a week.

Where pirates hunted in search of easy prey.

The crew of the *Mermaid* were not interested in slavers or the foetid coast. Their rough-voiced, ragged-faced captain, Malachias Taylor, had more lucrative things in mind – the sighting of another ship, preferably a full-laden, poorly manned merchantman with a rich cargo worth plundering.

"What can y'see?" he shouted from the deck, squinting upwards at his quartermaster, the relentless sun dazzling his eyes. His second-in-command, Jesamiah, like his father before him, was one of the best seamen Taylor knew.

"Nothing! If young Daniel here did see a sail he has better sight than

I 'ave," Jesamiah called down, the frustration clear in his voice. All the same, he studied the sea again with the telescope.

Jesamiah Acorne. Quick to smile, formidable when angered. Tall, tanned, with strong arms and a seaman's tar-stained and callused hands. His black hair fell as an untidy chaos of natural curls to his shoulders; laced into it, lengths of blue ribbons which streamed about his face in the wind, the whipping ends stinging his cheeks. The ladies ashore thought them a wonderful prize when he occasionally offered one as a keepsake.

If there was a ship, Daniel would only have glimpsed her highest sails, the topgallants; the rest of her would still be hull down, unseen below the curve of the horizon. "I think you had too much rum last night, my lad." Jesamiah grinned. "Your eyes are playing tricks on you."

Young Daniel was adamant. "I saw her, I say. I'll wager m'next wedge of baccy I did!"

"You know I cannot abide the stuff," Jesamiah chuckled good-naturedly as he stretched out his arm to ruffle the lad's mop of hair. He had turned his back on anything to do with tobacco – except stealing it – seven years ago when his elder brother had thrown him off their dead father's plantation, with the threat that he would hang if ever he returned. But then, Phillipe Mereno was only a half-brother and he had always been a cheat and a bully. One day, for the misery of his childhood, Jesamiah would find the opportunity to go back and finish beating the bastard to a pulp.

Out of habit, he touched the gold charm dangling from his right earlobe: an acorn, to match the signet ring he had worn since early youth. Presents from his Spanish mother, God rest her soul. She had always thought the acorn, the fruit of the solid and dependable oak tree, to be lucky. It had been the first word to come to mind when he had needed a new name in a hurry.

Acorne, with an "e" to make the name unique, and his own.

As Jesamiah was about to shut the telescope a flash caught his eye and he whisked the instrument upwards again. The sun reflecting on something?

"Wait… Damn it, Daniel – I've got her!" The sudden enthusiasm carried in an eager flurry as he shouted down to the deck, his words greeted by a hollered cheer from the rag-tag of men who made up the *Mermaid*'s crew.

Even the usually dour-faced Malachias Taylor managed a smile. "Probably a slaver," he muttered, "but we'll set all sail an' pay her a visit." His gap-toothed smile broadened into a grin. "She might be wantin' company, eh lads?"

Aye, she might, but not the sort of company the *Mermaid* would be offering. Respectable traders and East India merchantmen did not care for pirates.

Half an hour. Three-quarters. The sand trickled through the half-hour glass as if it were sticky with tar, and although the *Mermaid* was under full sail the distance between the two ships seemed to take an interminable time to lessen. Each man was trying to pretend he did not care whether they had a possible Prize or not, but, for all that, finding a variety of excuses to be on deck or clambering about the rigging. In the end, Jesamiah, back on the quarterdeck, put a stop to it, cursing them for the dregs they were.

"Looking ain't going to bring us closer to a Chase any the quicker!" he barked, resisting the temptation to have yet another squint through the telescope for himself. "Cease this 'opping about as if you've an army of ants crawling up yer backsides! We stay on this course and make out we're minding our own business. We ain't interested in her, savvy?" All the same, he touched his gold earring for luck.

From his high vantage point Daniel finally put them out of their misery. "On deck there! She's a trader!" he shouted. "A dirty, great, huge, East Indiaman – God's breath, would you believe it? There's something smaller following in her wake." He cursed again and spat chewed tobacco into the sea. "We wait all this damned time then get two Chases at once!"

The captain climbed aloft himself, a satisfied smile spread over his weatherworn face as he lifted the telescope to his eye. The Indiaman must have been keeping lookout too, for as he watched she showed her identity, the tri-coloured Dutch ensign clearly hoisted to her mainmast. Britain was not at war with the Dutch. A minor fact, which did not perturb Taylor in the slightest.

Privateering during periods of declared war was legal, providing the captain carried a Letter of Marque giving him government permission to harass enemy ships. Naturally, Captain Taylor possessed his formal letter, and, naturally, he preyed on any Spanish or French enemy ship daring to show a sail over the horizon. He saw no reason to ignore everything else also coming within range of his cannon, though, British or Dutch included. Now that was not privateering, but piracy – a crime punished by the death penalty of hanging.

"Show British colours, let her think we're friendly," he called down. He winked at Daniel. "We take the trader, put a scratch crew aboard then think about chasing after the other one as well, eh? What say you, young Wickersley?"

Daniel grinned a half-moon smile at Taylor, a fairer, more profitable captain than his previous one aboard an English Royal Navy frigate. "Aye, sir, sounds good t'me!"

Jesamiah was waiting for orders, his hand curled loosely around the hilt of his cutlass slung from a leather baldric worn aslant across his faded waistcoat, the strap concealing a rough-patched, bloodstained hole where some while ago a pistol's lead shot had penetrated. He wore canvas breeches as soft and comfortable as moleskin, knee-high boots and a cotton shirt that had once been white but was now a dirty grey. One cuff was beginning to fray into a ragged edge. He stood, his other hand fiddling with his blue ribbons, legs straddled, balancing against the rise and fall of the ship.

Taylor slid hand over hand down the backstay; watching him, Jesamiah ran his finger and thumb across the moustache trailing each side of his mouth into a beard trimmed close along his jaw. He lifted his chin slightly as Taylor's feet touched the deck. Taylor looked towards his second-in-command. "If you please, Mister Acorne."

Acknowledging, Jesamiah paused, knowing the crew of eighty rogues were set to jump at his command. He held them a moment... "All hands! Clear for action!"

A whoop of delight, a scuffing patter of bare feet on the sun-hot deck, the tarred caulking sticky between the boards, the men scattering in various directions to ready the ship for fighting. A task they could do day or night, drunk or sober.

As captain of a pirate ship, Taylor only held unquestionable command when it came to the engagement of an enemy ship. At other times decisions were made by discussion and a vote. And if a captain got it wrong too often? The crew simply elected another one.

Taylor was safe. He was skilled at piracy, his achievements obvious by his long standing as master of the *Mermaid* over a contented crew.

"Make ready the guns," he called to Jesamiah, "but don't run out yet. Keep some of the crew out o' sight, too. I want this

Dutchman thinkin' we're a poorly manned merchant, no threat, for as long as possible."

Jesamiah grinned, the light of easy laughter darting into his face. He wanted that too. The easier the chase and the fight at the end of it, the better.

He had no fear of dying, for everyone had to go eventually, hoped when his turn came it would be quick and painless, for it was the long, drawn-out agony he and any pirate, any man, dreaded. But today? This fine, clear blue day was not a day for dying.

This was a day for taking treasure!

CONTINUING THE SEA WITCH VOYAGES OF CAPTAIN JESAMIAH ACORNE

Sea Witch: The first voyage
Pirate Code: The second voyage
Bring It Close: The third voyage
Ripples In The Sand: The fourth voyage
On The Account: The fifth voyage

To Follow:

Gallows Wake: The sixth voyage
Jamaica Gold: The seventh voyage

When The Mermaid Sings: *a short novel prequel.*

HOW TO SAY 'THANK YOU' TO YOUR FAVOURITE AUTHORS

Leave a review on Amazon
http://viewauthor.at/HelenHollick

'Like' and 'follow' where you can
Subscribe to a newsletter
Buy a copy of your favourite book as a present
Spread the word!

MORE PIRATES!

Pirates have left a mark on cultures around the world. They've been the subject of stories for centuries. From pirate books like Helen's awesome *Sea Witch Voyages* to TV shows and board games.

Helen has teamed up with Green Feet Games and game designers, Dr Sam Hillier and Tom Butler who are expanding their Pirate Republic board game to encompass the West African coast and further piratical missions - which will include an adventure with Jesamiah Acorne and the crew of *Mermaid*.

You can find updates and developments here on Helen's Blog:

https://ofhistoryandkings.blogspot.com/p/pirates.html

ALSO BY HELEN HOLLICK

THE JAN CHRISTOPHER MURDER MYSTERY SERIES

A Mirror Murder

To follow

A Mystery of Murder

Murder by Mistake

THE PENDRAGON'S BANNER TRILOGY

The Kingmaking: Book One

Pendragon's Banner: Book Two

Shadow of the King: Book Three

THE SAXON 1066 SERIES

A Hollow Crown (UK edition title)

The Forever Queen (US edition title. USA Today bestseller)

Harold the King (UK edition title)

I Am The Chosen King (US edition title)

1066 Turned Upside Down (alternative short stories by various authors)

BETRAYAL

Short stories by various authors

NON-FICTION

Pirates: Truth and Tales

Life Of A Smuggler: In Fact And Fiction

Discovering The Diamond (with Jo Field)

PRAISE FOR HELEN HOLLICK'S NOVELS

"I sank into this gentle cosy mystery story with the same enthusiasm and relish as I approach a hot bubble bath, and really enjoyed getting to know the central character, a shy young librarian, and the young police officer who becomes her romantic interest." *Debbie Young*

"Helen Hollick has it all! She tells a great story, gets her history right, and writes consistently readable books" *Bernard Cornwell*

"A novel of enormous emotional power" *Elizabeth Chadwick*

"In the sexiest pirate contest, Cpt Jesamiah Acorne gives Jack Sparrow a run for his money!" *Sharon K. Penman*

"Thanks to Hollick's masterful storytelling Harold's nobility and heroism enthral to the point of engendering hope for a different ending to the famous battle of 1066" *Publisher's Weekly*

"If only all historical fiction could be this good" *Historical Novel Society*

"Most impressive" *The Lady*

9 781838 131869